Praise for Bernhard Schlink's

Summer Lies

"Schlink's ability to draw convincing portraits and believable scenes coupled with his refusal to bend his plots into neat packages make these stories true to life."   —*The Toronto Star*

"In each affecting story in this hot, blurry haze of summer, the valley between truth and deception is neither straight nor wide."   —*Booklist*

"A thoughtful, stimulating collection."
                —*Kirkus Reviews*

"Eloquent and profound. . . . A generally top-notch collection from Schlink."
                —*Publishers Weekly*

"Moving, atmospheric. . . . However shadowed, the life Mr. Schlink assiduously documents brims with hope."   —*The New York Journal of Books*

Bernhard Schlink

Summer Lies

Bernhard Schlink is the author of the internationally bestselling novel *The Reader*. He is a former judge and teaches law in Berlin and New York City.

INTERNATIONAL

Also by Bernhard Schlink

The Weekend

Homecoming

The Reader

Flights of Love

Self's Murder

Self's Deception

Self's Punishment *(with Walter Popp)*

Summer Lies

Bernhard Schlink

TRANSLATED FROM THE GERMAN BY
CAROL BROWN JANEWAY

Vintage International

VINTAGE BOOKS

A DIVISION OF RANDOM HOUSE, INC.

NEW YORK

FIRST VINTAGE INTERNATIONAL EDITION, MAY 2013

Translation copyright © 2012 by Carol Brown Janeway

The Library of Congress has cataloged the Pantheon edition as follows:
Schlink, Bernhard.
[Sommerlügen. English]
Summer lies / Bernhard Schlink ; translated from the German
by Carol Brown Janeway
p. cm.
1. Janeway, Carol Brown. II. Title.
PT2680.L54S6513 2012
833'.914–dc23   2012005994

Vintage ISBN: 978-0-307-94832-8

Book design by M. Kristen Bearse

www.vintagebooks.com

Printed in the United States of America
10 9 8 7 6 5 4 3 2

Contents

After the Season   3

The Night in Baden-Baden   37

The House in the Forest   68

Stranger in the Night   104

The Last Summer   138

Johann Sebastian Bach on Ruegen   174

The Journey to the South   195

Summer Lies

After the Season

1

They had to say goodbye in front of security.

But because it was a small airport, all the check-in desks and the control points were in the same hall, so he could follow her with his eyes as she set her bag on the conveyor belt, walked through the metal detector, showed her boarding pass, and was led to the plane, which was standing on the runway right outside the glass door.

She kept on looking back at him and waving. On the steps up to the plane she turned one last time, laughing and crying, and laid her hand on her heart. When she'd disappeared into the plane, he waved at the little windows, but didn't know if she could see him or not. Then the engines were started, the propellers turned, the plane began to roll, faster and faster, and took off.

His flight wasn't leaving for another hour. He got himself a cup of coffee and a newspaper and sat down on a bench. Since they had met, he hadn't read a newspaper anymore or sat alone over a cup of coffee. After a quarter of an hour, during which he still hadn't read a single line or swallowed a single mouthful, he thought, I've forgotten how to be alone. It was a thought he liked.

2

He had arrived thirteen days before. The season was over, and with it the good weather. It was raining, and he spent the afternoon with a book on the covered porch of his bed-and-breakfast. When he made himself go out into the bad weather the next day to walk along the beach in the rain to the lighthouse, he first encountered the woman on the way there, and then again on the way back. They smiled at each other, with curiosity at first, and then a hint of familiarity the second time around. They were the only two people out for a walk in the entire area, companions in both misfortune and pleasure: each of them would have preferred a clear blue sky, but enjoyed the soft rain.

In the evening she was sitting alone on the large terrace of the popular seafood restaurant with its plastic roof and windows already installed for fall. She had a full glass in front of her and was reading a book—a sign, perhaps, that she hadn't eaten yet and wasn't waiting for her husband or lover? He hesitated in the doorway until she looked up and smiled at him companionably. Then he took his courage in both hands, walked over to her table, and asked if he might join her.

"Please," she said, and laid her book aside.

He sat down, and because she had already ordered, she could make suggestions, and he chose the cod she had already picked out for herself. Then neither of them knew how to strike up a conversation. The book was no help; it was lying there in a way that made it impossible for him to read the title. Finally he said, "There's something about taking a late vacation on the Cape."

"Because the weather's so good?" She laughed.

Was she making fun of him? He looked at her, not a pretty face, eyes too small, chin too pronounced, but her expression wasn't mocking, it was cheerful, maybe even a little unsure. "Because you have the beach to yourself. Because you can get a table in restaurants that are impossible to get into during the season. Because you're less alone with a few people than you are with a crowd."

"Do you always come when the season's over?"

"It's my first time here. I should really be working. But my finger isn't back in shape yet, and it can do its exercises just as well here as in New York." He moved the little finger of his left hand up and down, curling it and stretching it out again.

She looked at the little finger, puzzled. "What is it exercising for?"

"For the flute. I play in an orchestra. And you?"

"I learned the piano but rarely ever play." She blushed. "That's not what you meant. I often came here with my parents when I was a child, and sometimes that makes me nostalgic. And after the season's over, the Cape has that magic you described. Everything is emptier and more peaceful—I like it."

He didn't say that a vacation during the season would be more than he could afford, and assumed it must be true for her as well. She wore sneakers, jeans, and a sweatshirt, and there was a faded waxed jacket on the back of her chair. When they studied the wine list together, she suggested a cheap bottle of sauvignon blanc. She talked about Los Angeles, about her work at a foundation that supported theater programs for children from the ghetto, about life with no winter, about the sheer might of the Pacific, about the traffic. He talked about tripping over a cable laid in the wrong place and breaking his finger, about breaking his arm when he jumped out of the window aged nine and breaking his leg while skiing aged thirteen. At first they sat alone on the terrace, then other guests came, and then they sat alone again over another bottle of wine. When they looked through the window, the sea and the beach were enveloped in utter darkness. The rain pattered on the roof.

"What are your plans for tomorrow?"

"I know you get breakfast in a bed-and-breakfast. But would you like to come over and have it with me?"

He walked her home. She took his arm under the umbrella. Neither of them spoke. Her little house was on the street that led to his bed-and-breakfast a mile further on. The light went on automatically over the front door, and suddenly when they looked at each other everything was too bright. She gave him a quick hug and the faintest breath of a kiss. Before she closed the door he said, "My name's Richard. What's . . . ?"

"I'm Susan."

3

Richard woke up early, folded his arms behind his head, and listened to the rain in the trees and on the gravel of the path outside. He liked the regular, soothing pattering sound, even if it didn't bode well for the day. Would he and Susan walk on the beach after breakfast? Or in the woods surrounding the lake? Or take a bike ride? He hadn't rented a car and guessed she hadn't either. So the radius of any excursion they might undertake together was limited.

He curled and stretched his little finger so as not to have to exercise that much later. He was feeling a little anxious. If Susan and he were actually going to spend the day together after breakfast and also eat together or maybe even cook— what came after that?

Must he sleep with her? Show her that she was a desirable woman and he was aroused by her? Because if he didn't he would upset her and embarrass himself? It was years since he'd slept with a woman. He didn't feel he was someone who was easily aroused, and hadn't found her very desirable on the previous evening. She had lots of things to tell, lots of questions to ask, she listened attentively, she was lively and witty. The way she always hesitated for a fraction of a second before she said something and squeezed her eyes when she was concentrating was charming. She aroused his interest. But his desire?

Breakfast had been set for him in the main room, and because he didn't want to disappoint the elderly couple who'd squeezed orange juice, whipped up scrambled eggs, and made pancakes, he sat down and ate. The wife came out of the kitchen every couple of minutes to ask if he'd care for more coffee or more butter or a different kind of jam or maybe some fruit or yoghurt. Finally he realized she wanted to talk to him. He asked her how long she'd lived here, and she set down the coffeepot and stood by the table. Forty years ago her husband had inherited a little money and they'd bought the house on the Cape, where he wanted to write and she wanted to paint. But neither the writing nor the painting came to anything, and when the children were grown and the inheritance had run out, they turned the house into a bed-and-breakfast. "Whatever you want to know about the Cape, the most beautiful spots and the best places to eat, just ask me. And if you're going out today—the beach is still the beach when it's raining, the woods are just wet."

In the woods, the mist hung in the trees. It also enveloped the houses that were set back from the road. The little house that Susan lived in was a porter's lodge; next to it was a driveway leading to a large, mist-shrouded, mysterious house. He couldn't find a bell, and so he knocked. "Coming," she yelled, and her voice sounded a long way away. He heard her running up some stairs, banging a door shut, and running along a corridor. Then she was standing in front of him, out of breath, clutching a bottle of champagne. "I was in the cellar."

The champagne made him anxious again. He saw himself sitting side by side with her on a sofa in front of a fire with their glasses. She slid closer to him. Had things gone that far already?

"Don't stand there staring. Come in!"

In the big room next to the kitchen he actually saw a fireplace with logs next to it and a sofa in front. Susan had laid the table in the kitchen and once again he drank orange juice and ate scrambled eggs and afterward there was fruit salad with nuts in it. "It tasted wonderful. But now I need to get out and run or ride a bike or swim." As she looked doubtfully at the rain, he explained about his double breakfast.

"You didn't want to disappoint John and Linda? That was so sweet of you!" She looked at him admiringly, pleased. "Yes, why not go swimming! You don't have bathing trunks? You want to . . ." She looked a bit doubtful, but acquiesced, packed towels into a large bag, and added an umbrella, the champagne, and two glasses. "We can walk across the property, it's a prettier route and faster, too."

4

They passed the big house with its tall pillars and closed shutters, as mysterious now as it had been at a distance. They climbed the broad steps, stood on the terrace between the columns, walked around the house, and found the stairway to the covered porch that circled the floor above. From here there was an overcast view across the dunes and the beach to the gray sea.

"It's absolutely calm," she whispered.

Could she see that at such a distance? Could she hear it?

It had stopped raining, and in the deep silence he too could do no more than whisper. "Where are the gulls?"

"Out on the waves. When the rain stops, the worms come out of the earth and the fish come up to the surface of the water."

"I don't believe it."

She laughed. "Didn't we want to have a swim?" She started to run, so fast and so sure of the way that he couldn't manage the big bag and keep up with her. He lost sight of her in the dunes, and as he reached the beach she was already pulling off the last sock and running toward the water. When he reached the sea she was swimming far out.

The water was indeed absolutely calm, and felt cold only until he started to swim. Then it stroked his naked body. He swam out a long way and then allowed himself to be carried, floating on his back. Susan was further out still, doing the crawl. When the rain began again, he enjoyed the drops falling on his face.

The rain got heavier, and he could no longer see Susan. He called out. He swam in the direction he thought he'd seen her last, and called out again. When he was almost no longer able to see land, he turned back. He wasn't a fast swimmer, and exerted himself to go faster but only made slow progress, and the slowness turned his anxiety into panic. How long would Susan hold out? Did he have his cell phone in the pocket of his pants? Would he be able to get a connection on the beach? Where was the nearest house? The anxiety was too much for him; he got slower and even more panicked.

Then he saw a pale figure climb out of the sea and stand on the beach. Anger gave him strength. How could she have inflicted such fear on him! When she waved, he didn't wave back.

When he was standing in front of her, furious, she smiled at him. "What's the matter?"

"What's the matter? I was petrified when I could no longer see you. Why didn't you swim close to me on your way back?"

"I didn't see you."

"You didn't see me?"

She went red. "I'm rather shortsighted."

His anger suddenly struck him as absurd. They were facing each other naked and wet, rain was dripping down both their faces, they both had goose bumps and were shivering and warming their chests with their arms. She looked at him with the vulnerable, searching look that he now knew wasn't uncertainty, just shortsightedness. He saw the blue veins in her thin white skin, her pubic hair, reddish blond although the hair on her head was pale blond, her flat stomach and narrow hips, her strong arms and legs. He was ashamed of his body, and pulled his stomach in. "I'm sorry I was so rough."

"I understand. You were afraid." She smiled again.

He was embarrassed. Then he gave himself a shake, jerked his head toward the place by the dunes where their things were lying, called "Go!," and started running. She was faster than he was and could have overtaken him effortlessly. But she ran beside him, and it reminded him of his childhood and the joy of running together toward some common goal with his sisters or his friends. He saw her small breasts, which she'd shielded with her arms when they'd been standing on the beach, and her small behind.

5

Their clothes were wet. But the towels had stayed dry in the bag and Susan and Richard wrapped themselves in them, sat down under the umbrella, and drank champagne.

She leaned against him. "Tell me about yourself from the beginning, about your mother and father and your siblings, and all the way to now. Were you born in America?"

"Berlin. My parents were music teachers, he taught piano and she taught violin and viola. There were four of us children, and I was allowed to go to the music high school, though my three sisters were far better than I was. It's what my father wanted; he couldn't bear the thought that I would fail the way he'd failed. So for him I went to the music high school, for him I became second flute in the New York Philharmonic, and one day for him I'll become first flute in another good orchestra."

"Are your parents still alive?"

"My father died seven years ago, my mother last year."

She thought. Then she asked, "If you hadn't become a flautist for your father, but had done what you wanted—what would you be?"

"Don't laugh at me. When first my father then my mother died, I thought, finally I'm free, I can do what I want. But they're still sitting in my head, talking at me. I would have to get out for a year, away from the orchestra, away from the flute, go running, go swimming, think about it all and maybe write about how it was at home with my parents and my sisters. So that at the end of a year I'd know what I want. Maybe it would even turn out to be the flute."

"I've sometimes wished someone would talk at me. My parents were killed in a car accident when I was twelve. The aunt I was sent to live with didn't like children. I also don't know if my father liked me. He sometimes said he looked forward to the time when I'd be older and he'd be able to see if he could make anything of me—didn't sound good."

"I'm sorry. How was your mother?"

"Beautiful. She wanted me to turn out as beautiful as she was. My clothes were as fine as Mother's, and when she helped me dress, she was wonderful, so affectionate and gentle. She could have taught me how to deal with mean girlfriends, pushy boyfriends, but I had to learn that on my own."

They sat under the umbrella, given over to their memories. Like two children who've got lost and are yearning for home, he thought. He thought of some of the favorite books of his childhood, in which boys and girls got lost and survived in caves and huts, or were attacked on a journey and dragged off into slavery, or kidnapped in London and forced to beg or steal, or sold from their homes in Ticino to become chimney sweeps in Milan. He had mourned with the children over the loss of their parents and shared their hopes of being reunited with them. But the appeal of the stories was that the children coped without their parents. When finally they came home, they had outgrown them. Why is it hard to be self-sufficient, even though all you need is yourself, nobody else? He sighed.

"What is it?"

"Nothing," he said, and put his arm around her.

"You sighed."

"I'd like to be further along than I am."

She snuggled against his side. "I know that feeling. But don't we make progress in fits and starts? Nothing happens for a long time, then suddenly we get a surprise, have an encounter, reach a decision point, and we're no longer the same as we were before."

"Not the same as we were before? Six months ago I was at a class reunion, and the people who'd been decent and nice when we were in school were still decent and nice, and the assholes were still assholes. The others must have had the same reaction to me. And it gave me a shock. You work on yourself, you think you're changing and developing, and then the others immediately recognize you as the person you always were."

"You Europeans are pessimists. You come from the Old World and can't imagine that there can be a New World and that people can make themselves new too."

"Let's take a walk along the beach. The rain's almost stopped."

They wrapped the towels around themselves and walked over the sand at the water's edge. They were barefoot, and the cold, wet sand prickled.

"I'm not a pessimist. I'm always hoping my life will get better."

"Me too."

When the rain got heavier again, they went back to Susan's house. They were freezing. While Richard took a shower, Susan went down to the cellar and turned on the heat; while Susan showered, Richard made a fire in the fireplace. He had put on Susan's father's bathrobe, which she had kept, red, warm, made of heavy wool lined with silk. They hung up their wet clothes to dry and figured out how to make the samovar that stood on the mantelpiece above the fireplace work. Then they sat on the sofa, she in one corner, cross-legged, he with his legs folded under him in the other, drank tea, and looked at each other.

"I'm sure my clothes will be ready to put on again soon."

"Stay. What are you going to do in the rain? Sit alone in your room?"

"I . . ." He wanted to add that he didn't want to impose, be a burden on her, mess up her day. But these were meaning-less phrases. He knew that his company gave her pleasure. He read it in her face and heard it in her voice. He smiled at her, politely at first, and then embarrassed. What if the situation was arousing expectations in Susan that he couldn't satisfy? But then she pulled a book out of the many piled along with newspapers beside the sofa and began to read. She sat reading so self-sufficiently, so comfortably, so relaxedly that he began to relax too. He looked for a book, found one that interested him, but didn't begin it: instead he watched her read, till she looked up and smiled at him. He smiled back, finally free of all tension, and began reading.

6

When he reached the bed-and-breakfast at ten p.m., Linda and John were sitting in front of the television. He told them he wouldn't be needing any breakfast next morning because he'd be having it with the young woman in the little house a mile further down the road, whom he'd got to know over dinner in the restaurant.

"She doesn't live in the big house?"

"She doesn't do it if she comes alone, and hasn't done it for a long time now."

"But last year . . ."

"Last year she came alone, but always had visitors."

Richard listened to Linda and John with mounting irritation. "You're talking about Susan . . ." He realized they'd introduced themselves to each other only with their first names.

"Susan Hartman."

"She owns the big house with the pillars?"

"Her grandfather bought it in the twenties. After her parents died the administrator ran down the estate, collected the rent, and invested nothing until Susan fired him a few years ago and restored the houses and the garden."

"Didn't that cost a fortune?"

"It didn't cause her any pain. Those of us who live here are happy—there were people interested in parceling up the land and dividing the house or replacing it with a hotel. It would have changed the entire area."

Richard said good night to Linda and John and went up to his room. He would not have started talking to Susan if he'd known how rich she was. He didn't like rich people. He despised inherited wealth and considered earned riches to be ill-gotten. His parents had never earned enough to give their four children the things they would have liked, and his salary from the New York Philharmonic was only just enough to cover his costs in the expensive city. He had no rich friends either now or earlier in his life.

He was furious with Susan. As if she'd led him around by the nose. As if she'd lured him into the situation in which he was now stuck. But was he stuck? He didn't have to go have breakfast with her the next day. Or he could go and tell her they couldn't see each other anymore, they were too different, their lives were too different, their worlds were too different. But they had just spent the afternoon together in front of the fire, reading sentences aloud to each other from time to time, they had cooked together, eaten, washed up, watched a movie, and both of them had felt good. Too different?

He brushed his teeth so furiously that he hurt his left cheek. He sat down on the bed with his hand to his cheek, feeling sorry for himself. He really was stuck. He had fallen in love with Susan. Only a little, he told himself. For what did he really know about her? What actually did he like about her? How would things go, given the difference in their lives and their worlds? Perhaps she would find it charming to eat three times in the little Italian restaurant he could afford. After that, should he allow her to invite him out instead? Or should he run up debt on credit cards?

He didn't sleep well. He kept waking up, and around six a.m., when he realized he wouldn't go to sleep again, he gave up, put on his clothes, and left the house. The sky was filled with dark clouds, but there was a red glow in the east. If Richard wasn't to miss the sunrise over the ocean he'd have to hurry and run in his regular shoes, which he'd put on instead of his running shoes. The soles made a loud noise on the road, once scaring up a flock of crows and once several hares. In the east the red was glowing brighter and stronger; Richard had seen a sunset like that before, but never such a sunrise. As he passed Susan's house he took care to move quietly.

Then he reached the beach. The sun came up golden out of a molten sea and into a sky that was all flames—it was a matter of moments, and then the clouds extinguished everything. Richard suddenly felt as if it wasn't just darker but colder.

He needn't have bothered to be quiet in front of Susan's house. She too was already up, sitting at the foot of a dune. She saw him, got to her feet, and came toward him. She moved slowly: the sand by the dunes was deep and made walking difficult. Richard went to meet her, but only because he wished to be polite. He preferred to just watch her as she walked calmly and confidently, her head sometimes down and then raised, and when it was raised her eyes were always on his face. It felt as if they were negotiating something, but he didn't know what it was. He didn't understand what question was in her eyes or what answers she found in his. He smiled but she didn't smile back, just looked at him gravely.

When they stood facing each other, she took his hand. "Come!" She led him to her house and upstairs into the bedroom. She undressed, lay down on the bed, and watched as he undressed and lay down beside her. "I've waited such a long time for you."

7

That was the way she made love to him. As if she had been searching for him forever and had finally found him. As if neither she nor he could do anything wrong.

She swept him along, and he allowed it to happen. He didn't ask himself: How am I? And didn't ask her: How was I? As they lay next to each other afterward, he knew that he loved her. This little person with eyes that were too small and a chin that was too pronounced, skin that was too thin, and a figure more like a boy's than the womanly shapes he had loved until now. With a confidence that after being pushed around from only moderately loving parents to a loveless aunt she had no right to have. With more money than could be good for her. And who saw something in him that he didn't see himself, and thereby made a gift of it to him.

For the first time, he had made love to a woman as if no images existed of how love was supposed to take place. As if they were a couple out of the nineteenth century, for whom the movies and television could not yet dictate the right way to kiss, the right way to moan, the right way for the face to express passion and the body to shudder with desire. A couple who were discovering love and kissing and moaning for themselves. Susan didn't seem to close her eyes once. Whenever he looked at her, she was also looking at him. He loved that look, faraway, trusting.

She propped herself up and laughed at him. "Thank good-ness I smiled at you in the restaurant when you didn't know what to do. At first I didn't think it was necessary. I thought you'd come to me as directly and quickly as you could."

He happily echoed her laugh. It didn't occur to them to take the clumsy, grating aspects of their meeting in the restaurant as any kind of warning. They took it as an awkwardness that laughter could dispel.

They stayed in bed until evening. Then they opened the garage and took Susan's car, a well-maintained elderly BMW, to drive through rain and darkness to a supermarket. The light was harsh, it smelled of cleaning fluids, the music was synthetic, and the handful of customers were wearily pushing their carts through the empty aisles. "We should have stayed in bed," she whispered to him, and he was glad that she was as disturbed by the light and the smell and the music as he was. She sighed, laughed, started shopping, and soon had filled up her cart. From time to time he added something, apples, pan-cake mix, wine. At the checkout, he paid with his credit card and knew that next month, for the first time, he wouldn't be able to pay in full. It made him uncomfortable, but more than that, it irritated him that on a day like today something as triv-ial as an overdrawn credit account could upset him. So in the wine and liquor section he bought three bottles of champagne for good measure.

On the way home she asked, "Shall we get your things?"

"Maybe Linda and John are already asleep. I don't want to wake them."

Susan nodded. She drove fast and with assurance, and by the way she took the many curves, he could tell that she knew the car and the route well. "Did you drive the car here from Los Angeles?"

"No, the car belongs here. Clark takes care of the house and the garden and the car as well."

"You only stay in the big house when you have guests?"

"Shall we move up there tomorrow?"

"I don't know. It's . . ."

"It's too big for me. But with you there it would be fun. We'd read in the library, play billiards in the billiards room, you could practice the flute in the music room, and I'd have breakfast served in the little salon and dinner in the big one." She talked more and more happily, more and more firmly. "We'll sleep in the big bedroom where my grandparents and parents slept. Or we'll sleep in my room in the bed where I dreamed of my prince when I was a girl."

He saw her smiling face in the dull glow of the dashboard. Susan was lost in her memories. For the first time since they'd met, she was somewhere else. Richard wanted to ask which actor or singer she'd dreamed of back then, wanted to know everything about the men in her life, wanted to hear that they'd all been mere prophets while he was the Messiah. But then he thought that his worries about the other men were as petty as the excessive charge on his credit account. He was tired and laid his head on Susan's shoulder. She reached over and stroked his head with her left hand, pressed his head to her shoulder, and he fell asleep.

8

Over the next few days he learned everything about the men in Susan's life. He also learned about her longing for children, at least two, preferably four. At first with her husband there was no success, then she no longer loved him and she got divorced.

He learned she'd studied art history at college, then had gone to business school, and had reorganized a toy train manufacturer which she'd inherited from her father and then sold along with the other firms she'd inherited. He learned that she had an apartment in Manhattan that she was in the process of having renovated because she wanted to move from Los Angeles to New York. He also learned that she was forty-one, two years older than he was.

Again and again, whatever Susan told him about her life until now ended in plans for their future together. She described her apartment in New York: the wide staircase in the duplex that led up from the sixth floor to the seventh, the wide corridors, the large high rooms, the kitchen with the dumbwaiter, the view of the park. She had grown up in the apartment until her aunt fetched her to Santa Barbara after her parents' death. "I used to slide down the banisters and roller-skate in the corridors, I could get into the dumbwaiter till I was six, and when I was in bed I could watch the tops of the trees waving from out of my window. You have to go see the apartment!" She couldn't show it to him herself because she was flying back from the Cape to Los Angeles to organize both the foundation's move and her own. "Will you meet with the architect? We can still change everything."

Her grandfather had acquired not only the duplex but the entire building on Fifth Avenue at a very favorable price during the Depression. Along with the estate on the Cape and another in the Adirondacks. "I have to renovate that again too. Do you enjoy architecture? Building and renovating and decorating? I got the plans and brought them with me—shall we look at them together?"

She talked about a couple, old friends of hers, who had been trying in vain to have children for years, and had just spent their vacation at a fertility farm. She described the diet and the program, which laid out when the two of them were to sleep, exercise, eat, even have sex. She found it funny, but was also a little anxious. "You Europeans don't know about this kind of thing, or so I read. You see life as fate that cannot be changed."

"Yes," he said, "and if we're destined to kill our fathers and sleep with our mothers, there's nothing we can do about it."

She laughed. "Then you really can't hold anything against the fertility farm. If it doesn't help your destiny, it can't do any harm, either." She shrugged apologetically. "It's just because things didn't work with Robert back then. Perhaps it wasn't my fault, perhaps he was the one with the problem, we didn't have any tests done. But all the same, I've been afraid ever since."

He nodded. He was feeling afraid too. About the minimum two, maximum four children. And beforehand, about having to follow a set diet and have sex at set times with Susan at the fertility farm. About the loud ticking of the biological clock until the fourth child arrived or no more children were possible. About the possibility that Susan's abandon and passion when she made love to him weren't about him at all.

"Don't be afraid. I just say what's on my mind. That doesn't mean it's my last word on anything. You censor what you say.

"Again, that's European."

He didn't want a conversation about his fear. She was right: he censored what he said, while she said directly whatever she was thinking or feeling. No, she didn't want to plan a visit with him to the fertility farm. But she did want to plan the future with him, and although he too wanted it more with every day that passed, he had so much less to bring to the relationship than she did: no apartment, no houses, no money. If he and the woman at the first desk of the second violin section had fallen in love, then they would have looked for an apartment together and decided together which of his furniture and which of her furniture would go into the new apartment and what they would have to find at a thrift store. Susan was certainly ready to fill a room or two with his furniture. But he knew it wouldn't fit in.

He'd be able to bring his flute and his sheet music, and practice at the music stand that would certainly exist among all her furniture. He could put his books in her bookcases, order his papers in her father's filing cabinet, and write his letters at her father's desk. He would best leave his clothes in the closet here in the country; in the city, he wouldn't look so good in them when he was with her. She would be delighted to use her sense of fashion to buy him new ones.

He practiced a lot. Most of the time "dry," as he called it, when he simply curled and stretched his little finger. But more and more frequently on the flute itself. It was becoming a part of him in a way it never had before. It belonged to him, it was worth a lot, with it he created music and made money, he could take it wherever he went, he was at home with it anywhere. And when he played, he offered Susan something that no one else could offer her. When he improvised, he made melodies that fit her moods.

9

The corner room in the big house was their favorite. The many windows reached down to the floor and could be slid aside in good weather and protected with shutters when it was bad. When rain prevented them from walking on the beach, this was where they could still feel in touch with the ocean, the waves, the seagulls, and the occasional passing ship. Sometimes when they were out on the sand, the cold rain lashed their faces so sharply that it hurt.

The room was furnished with cane recliners, big chairs and tables, with soft cushions against the hard-woven surfaces. "Pity," he said when she led him through the house and he saw the recliners, which were only wide enough for one person. Two days later, as they were having breakfast in the little salon, a truck pulled up and two men in blue coveralls carried a double recliner into the house. It matched the other furniture, and the cushions had the same flower pattern as the other cushions.

The weather made every day like every other. It rained day after day, sometimes rising to the level of a storm, sometimes stopping for hours or sometimes mere minutes, and sometimes the skies cleared for a moment and the rooftops made sheets of light. When the weather allowed, Susan and Richard walked on the beach; if they ran out of supplies they drove to the supermarket, otherwise they stayed in the big house. When they switched from the little house to the big one, Susan had called Clark's wife, Mita, who came for a few hours every day to take care of cleaning and washing and cooking. She was so discreet that it was several days before Richard met her.

One evening they invited Linda and John to dinner. Susan and Richard cooked, having no idea how, so that they even found it difficult to follow the cookbook. But they finally managed to serve steaks with potatoes and salad and felt good about being able to cope in a crisis together. Apart from this they invited no one, nor did they visit other people. "There'll still be time for our friends."

When dusk came, they made love. The evening light sufficed them until it was totally dark, when they lit a candle. They made love so peacefully that Richard sometimes wondered if he'd make Susan happier by ripping off the clothes of both of them, throwing himself on her, and surrendering himself to her. He didn't manage to try, and she didn't seem to miss it. We're not feral cats, he thought, we're house cats.

Until they had their big fight, the first and the only one. They were going to go to the supermarket, and Susan kept Richard waiting in the car because she had to take a sudden phone call, which went on forever. That she let him wait without any explanation, that she had forgotten him or could simply neglect him, made him so angry that he got out, went into the house, and attacked her just as she put down the receiver. "Is this what I have to expect? What you do is important and what I do isn't? Your time is precious and mine doesn't count?"

At first she didn't understand. "Los Angeles called. The chairman . . ."

"Why didn't you tell me? Why do you always . . ."

"I'm sorry I kept you waiting for a few minutes. I thought a European man sees . . ."

"The Europeans—I've had it up to here with your Europeans. I was waiting out there for half an hour . . ."

Now she got angry too. "Half an hour? It was a minute or two. If that's too long for you, go into the house and read the newspaper. You prima donna, you . . ."

"Prima donna? Me? Which of us . . ."

She accused him of making an incomprehensible, exaggerated to-do. He didn't understand what was supposed to be incomprehensible and exaggerated about wanting to count as much as she did, when he had nothing and she had everything. She didn't understand how he could be so absurd as to think that he didn't count. By the end they were yelling at each other in fury and despair.

"I hate you!" She advanced on him, he moved back, she kept coming, and when he was against the wall and could move no further, she beat his chest with her fists till he took her in his arms and held her tight. At first she fumbled at the buttons of his shirt, then tore it open, he tried to pull off her jeans and she his, but it was too cumbersome and went too slowly, so they each did their own, yanking off jeans and underpants and socks in a single motion. They had sex on the floor in the hall, fast, urgent, passionate.

Afterward he lay on his back with her half in the curve of his arm and half against his chest. "Well," he said, and laughed aloud. She made a slight movement, a shake of the head, a tiny shrug of the shoulders, and pressed herself closer to him. He sensed that unlike him, she hadn't made the transition from passionate fighting into passionate sex. She hadn't torn open his shirt because she wanted to feel his chest, she'd torn it open because she wanted to find his heart. The object of passion had been a return to the peace she had lost during their fight.

They drove to the supermarket and Susan filled up the cart as if they were staying for weeks. On the way home the sun broke through the clouds and they took the next road to the sea, not the open ocean but the bay. The water was unruffled and the sky clear; they could see the tip of the Cape and the other side of the bay.

"I like it before a storm when you can see so far and the contours are so sharp."

"Storm?"

"Yes. I don't know whether it's the humidity or the electricity that makes the air so clear, but it's the kind of air you get before a storm. Treacherous air: it promises you good weather and what you get is a storm."

"Please forgive me for attacking you before. And I didn't just attack you, I yelled at you too. I'm truly sorry."

He waited for her to say something. Then he saw that she

was crying and stood still, shocked. She lifted her tearstained face and put her arms around his neck. "No one has ever said anything as nice to me before. That he's sorry for what he said to me. I'm sorry too. I yelled too, I cursed you, and I hit you. We're never going to do that again, do you hear me? Never."

10

Then it was the last day. She was flying at four thirty, and he was flying at five thirty, and they ate a quiet breakfast on the terrace for the first time. The sun was so hot that it was as if the rain and the cold had just been an infection from which the summer had recovered again. Then they took a walk on the beach.

"It's only a few weeks."

"I know."

"Will you remember the appointment with the architect tomorrow?"

"Yes."

"And will you remember the mattress?"

"I haven't forgotten any of it. I'll buy a temporary mattress and cardboard furniture and plastic cutlery and dishes. If I have time, I'll go to the storage place and see if I like any of your parents' stuff. We'll furnish it all together, piece by piece. I love you."

"This is where we met the first day."

"Yes, on the way there. And over there again on the way back."

They talked about how they'd met, how unlikely their meetings had been, because it would have been so much more natural for him to be heading in one direction and she in another, how they could have failed to connect in the seafood restaurant that evening if she hadn't smiled at him, no, if he hadn't looked her way, how she had found him, no, he had found her.

"Shall we pack and then open the windows in the corner room? We still have a few hours."

"You don't have to pack much. Leave your summer clothes and your beach things here, then they'll be waiting for you next year."

He nodded. Although Linda and John had repaid him part of the money he'd paid in advance, his credit card charges were way over the limit. But the idea that he would have to buy more clothes in New York to replace what he was leaving here, thus running up his debt further, no longer scared him. That was how things were when you loved someone above your financial station. He would find a solution.

With the packed suitcases standing by the door, the house felt strange. They climbed the steps as they had done so often. But they trod carefully and spoke in hushed voices.

They slid the windows open and heard the breaking of the waves and the cries of the gulls. The sun was still shining, but Richard fetched the coverlet from the bedroom and spread it over the double recliner.

"Come!"

They undressed and slipped under the coverlet.

"How am I going to sleep without you?"

"And I without you?"

"Can you really not fly to Los Angeles with me?"

"I have rehearsals. Can you really not come to New York with me?"

She laughed. "Should I buy the orchestra? And then you schedule the rehearsals?"

"You can't buy the orchestra that quickly."

"Should I call?"

"Stay!"

They were afraid of saying goodbye, and at the same time its imminence made them curiously lighthearted. They were no longer in their shared life and not yet in their individual lives again: they were in no-man's-land. And that was how they made love, a little shyly at first, because they were becoming less familiar to each other again, and then serenely. As always she looked at him throughout, lost to the world, trusting.

They drove to the airport in Susan's car. Clark would collect it and drive it back. They exchanged details of when they would be where and how they could be reached, as if neither of them had a cell phone on which they could be reached anytime, anywhere. They told each other what they were going to be doing in the days and weeks until they were together again, and from time to time they played with ideas of this and that to do together in the future. The closer they came to the airport, the more Richard felt compelled to say something to Susan that would stay with her and keep her company. But he couldn't think of the right thing. "I love you," he said over and over again. "I love you."

11

He would have liked to see the house and the beach one more time from the plane. But they lay to the north, and the flight was headed southwest. He looked down at sea and islands, then Long Island, and finally Manhattan. The plane flew in a big turn as far as the Hudson and he recognized the church that stood only a few steps from his apartment.

It had been hard to get used to his neighborhood. It was noisy, and at the beginning when he came home past the cool, tough kids sitting out on the stoops in front of the houses or leaning on the railings drinking and smoking and playing loud music, he hadn't felt safe. Sometimes they said things to him and he didn't understand what they wanted and why they looked at him so truculently and laughed at him mockingly once he'd passed them by. Once they blocked his path and wanted his flute case—he thought they wanted to steal the flute, but they just wanted to see it and hear it. They switched off the music and were suddenly ill at ease in the ensuing silence. He was ill at ease too and still anxious on top of it, and first the flute sounded thin, but then he got braver and more at ease and the kids hummed the melody and clapped to the rhythm. Afterward he drank a beer with them. Since then they always hailed him with "Hey, pipe," or "Hola, flauta," and he greeted them back and gradually learned their names.

His apartment was noisy too. He heard his neighbors fighting, hitting one another, and having sex, and he knew their favorite programs on TV and the radio. One night he heard a shot fired in the building and for the next few days he eyed everyone he passed on the staircase suspiciously. When a neighbor invited him to a party, he tried to match up the people to the noises: the thin-lipped woman to the bickering voice, the man with the tattoos to the blows, the large daughter and her boyfriend to the sounds of sex. Once a year he repaid the invitations by giving a party himself, at which those neighbors, who hated one another, managed to behave well for his sake. He was never given any grief for his flute playing; he could practice early in the mornings and late at night, and wouldn't have disturbed anyone even at midnight. He always slept with earplugs.

The neighborhood changed over the years. Young couples

renovated run-down houses and transformed empty stores into restaurants. Richard met neighbors who were doctors, lawyers, and bankers, and could take his visitors out to a proper dinner. His building was one of the ones that remained as they were; the heirs who owned it were too conflicted among themselves to sell it or work on it. But he liked it that way. He liked the noises. They gave him the feeling that he was living in the real world, not just a rich enclave.

He became aware that when he'd described the next days and weeks to Susan, he'd left out the second oboe. They met weekly for dinner at the Italian restaurant on the corner, talked about life as Europeans in America, their professional hopes and disappointments, orchestra gossip, women—the oboist came from Vienna and found American women as difficult as Richard had up to now. He had also left out the old man who lived on the top floor of his building and sometimes came down in the evening for a game of chess with him and played so imaginatively and profoundly that Richard never minded always losing. He hadn't told her about Maria, one of the kids from the street, who had somehow got hold of a flute, had him show her how to hold it and put it to her mouth and read the music and kissed him on the lips and gave him a full-body hug when she said goodbye. Nor had he told her about Spanish lessons with the exiled Salvadoran teacher who lived on the next street over, nor about the decrepit fitness center where he felt comfortable. All he had described to Susan were the orchestra rehearsals and performances, the flautist who practiced with him from time to time, the children of the aunt who'd emigrated to New Jersey with a GI after the war, the fact that he was learning Spanish but not with whom, and that he went to a fitness center, but not where. He hadn't intended to keep secrets from her. It had just happened that way.

12

The taxi set him down in front of his building. It was warm, mothers with their babies were sitting out on the stoops, children were playing hide-and-seek between the parked cars, old men had set up folding chairs and brought cans of beer with them, a few boys were trying to walk as if they were grown up, and some girls were watching them and giggling. "Hola, flauta," his neighbor greeted him, "back from your trip?"

Richard looked up and down the street, sat down on the steps, put his suitcase next to him, and propped his arms on his knees. This was his world: the street, the neat houses and the shabby ones, the Italian restaurant on one corner where he met the oboist and at the other corner the street with the food shops, the newsstand, and the fitness center, and above the buildings the towers of the church that was next door to his Spanish teacher. He hadn't just got used to this world. He loved it. Since coming to New York, he hadn't had any lasting relationship with a woman. What kept him there was work, his friends, the people who lived on the street and in the buildings, the routine of shopping for groceries, going to the gym, always eating in the same restaurants. A day spent fetching the newspapers in the morning and exchanging three sentences about the weather with Amir, the owner of the newsstand, then reading the paper in the café, where they'd learned to bring him two soft-boiled eggs in a glass with chives and whole-wheat toast for breakfast, then practicing for a few hours before cleaning the apartment or doing the laundry, then exercising, then teaching Maria and getting a hug, then eating spaghetti Bolognese at the Italian place, then having a game of chess before going to bed—a day like that left nothing to be desired.

He looked at the building and up at the windows of his apartment. The morning glories were flowering; maybe Maria had actually watered them. He had started with window boxes, and now they were climbing in front of several of the windows. Had Maria also checked the bucket that collected the drips from the broken pipe? He would have to get it repaired, he hadn't had time to take care of it before he left on his trip.

He got to his feet, intending to go upstairs. But then he sat down again. Pulling the mail out of his box, climbing the stairs, unlocking the door, airing out the apartment, unpacking his bag, going through his mail and answering one or two e-mails, then taking a hot shower, throwing his dirty clothes into the laundry basket and getting clean clothes out of the cupboard, then finding a message on his answering machine from the oboist asking if he'd like to meet up tonight and calling him back to say yes—if he stepped back into his old life again it would never let go of him.

What had he been thinking? That he could carry his old life into a new life with Susan? That he could cross the city several times a week to go to the fitness center and his Spanish lesson? That then he would have chance encounters with Maria and the kids? That the old man from his building would occasionally take a taxi to the duplex on Fifth Avenue and play a game of chess with him in the drawing room under a genuine Gerhard Richter? That the oboist would feel comfortable in a restaurant on the East Side? He had had good reason to keep quiet with Susan about all the sides of his life he couldn't bring into their life together. He hadn't wanted to confront the fact that the new life would require him giving up the old one.

So? He loved Susan. He had had her all those days on the

Cape and had felt that nothing was lacking. And he would have her here now, and he would feel that nothing was lacking here either. The time they'd spent on the Cape hadn't just been wonderful because his own life was so far away! His life couldn't come between them here just because it found its recognizable form two miles from the location of the new life!

But yes, it could. So he mustn't go upstairs, he must go away, leave his old life behind, set out for the new life instead, right here, right now. Find a hotel. Camp out in Susan's apartment among the painters' ladders and their cans of paint. Arrange for someone to get all his things from his apartment and bring them to him. But the thought of a hotel room or Susan's apartment made him anxious, and he felt homesick even though he hadn't even left yet.

If only he were still on the Cape with Susan! If only her apartment were ready and she were here! If only lightning would strike his building and it would go up in flames!

He made a bet with himself. If someone went into the building in the next ten minutes, he would go in too; if no one did, then he'd take his suitcase and move to a hotel on the East Side. After fifteen minutes no one had entered the building, and he was still sitting on the steps. He tried it again. If in the next fifteen minutes an empty taxi drove down the street, he would take it and go to a hotel on the East Side, and if it didn't, he would go up to his apartment. Barely a minute later an empty taxi came along, but he didn't take it, nor did he go upstairs.

He admitted to himself that he couldn't cope on his own. He was also ready to admit it to Susan. He needed her help. She had to come to him and stay with him. She had to help him empty his old apartment and she had to settle into the new one with him. She could go to Los Angeles afterward. He called her. She was sitting in Boston in the lounge, but boarding had begun.

"I'm about to get onto the flight to Los Angeles."

"I need you."

"I need you too. My darling, I miss you so much!"

"No, I really need you. I can't cope with my old life and our new life together. You have to come, and go to Los Angeles later. Please!" There was a crackle in the receiver. "Susan? Can you hear me?"

"I'm on my way to the gate. Are you coming to Los Angeles?"

"No, Susan, you need to come to New York, I beg you."

"I wish I could come, I wish I were with you." He heard her being asked for her boarding pass. "Perhaps we can see each other next weekend, let's talk about it on the phone, I have to board now, I'm the last one. I love you."

"Susan!"

But she'd hung up, and when he called again, he was connected to her mailbox.

13

It got dark. The neighbor came to sit with him. "Problems?"

Richard nodded.

"Women?"

Richard laughed and nodded again.

"Understand." The neighbor stood up and left. Shortly afterward he came back, set a bottle of beer down next to Richard, and put a hand on his shoulder. "Drink!"

Richard drank and watched the bustle on the street. The kids a few buildings along, smoking and drinking and blasting their music. The dealer in the shadow of the steps, silently handing out little folded pieces of paper and pocketing dollar bills. The lovers in the doorway of the building. The old man, the last one left, who hadn't yet folded up his chair to carry it upstairs and got himself a can of beer out of his cooler from time to time. It was still warm; there was none of the sharpness in the air that can signal the nearness of fall on a late-summer evening; rather, it held the promise of a long, gentle end to the summer.

Richard was tired. He still had the feeling that he must choose between his old life and the new one, that he had to have the right idea or the necessary courage and then he would stand up as if involuntarily and either go upstairs or drive away. But the feeling was tired, just as he was.

Why should he take a taxi to a hotel on the East Side today? Why not tomorrow? Why should he not stay in his old life until he devoted himself to the new one? It would be laughable if in a few weeks he couldn't manage to switch out of his old life and into the new one. Could do it now. If he had to. But he didn't have to. Besides, nothing was to stop him going there now and coming back tomorrow. If he went later, he would never come back. The new life with Susan would hold him there.

What was important was to decide. And he had decided. He would give up his old life and start a new one with Susan. As soon as he could begin it properly. He couldn't do that yet. He would do it as soon as things were that far along. He would do it because he'd decided to. He would do it. Just not yet.

When he stood up, his arms and legs hurt. He stretched and looked around. The kids were at home, watching TV or playing with their computers or asleep. The street was empty.

Richard took his suitcase, unlocked the front door, collected the mail from the mailbox, climbed the stairs, and unlocked the door to his apartment. The bucket that collected the drips from the broken pipe was almost empty, and there was a bunch of asters on the table. Maria. The oboist was asking on the answering machine if they were going to see each other this evening. His Spanish teacher said hello on a postcard from his yoga vacation in Mexico. Richard switched on his computer, then switched it off again; the e-mails could wait. He unpacked, undressed, and threw his dirty clothes in the laundry basket.

He stood in the room naked, listening to the noises in the building. It was quiet next door; upstairs a TV murmured gently. From somewhere way below him in the building came the sounds of an argument, till a door slammed with a crash. Air conditioners hummed in several windows. The building was asleep.

Richard switched off the light and went to bed. Before he went to sleep he thought of Susan standing on the steps up to the plane, laughing and crying.

The Night in Baden-Baden

1

He took Therese with him, because that's what she'd been hoping. Because she was so happy about it. Because when she was happy she was a wonderful companion. Because there was no good reason not to take her.

It was the premiere of his first play. He was to sit in the box and walk onstage at the end and allow himself to be applauded or booed with the actors and the director. It was true that he didn't feel he deserved to be booed for a production he hadn't overseen himself. But he did want to stand onstage and be applauded.

He had booked a double room in Brenners Park-Hotel, where he had never been before. He looked forward to the luxuriousness of the room and the bathroom and to being able to wander through the park before the performance and take a seat on the veranda to enjoy a cup of Earl Grey and a club sandwich. They left in the early afternoon, made it onto the Autobahn in good time despite the Friday-afternoon traffic, and by four p.m. were already in Baden-Baden. First she took a bath in the tub with the gold fixtures, then he did. Afterward they wandered through the park and after the Earl Grey and the club sandwiches on the veranda, they drank champagne. Being together was pleasantly relaxing.

But she wanted more from him than he wanted from her or could give her. That's why for a whole year she hadn't wanted to see him, but then she missed their evenings together going to the movies or the theater or out to dinner, and accepted that all they ended with was a fleeting good-night kiss at her front door. Sometimes she snuggled up against him in the movie house, and sometimes he put his arm around her shoulders. Sometimes she took his hand when they were walking, and then sometimes he would hold hers tightly in his. Did she see in this a promise of greater possibilities between them? He wanted to keep things vague.

They went to the theater and were greeted by the director, introduced to the actors, and taken to their box. Then the curtain went up. He didn't recognize his play. The night during which a terrorist on the run takes refuge with his parents, his sister, and his brother was a travesty onstage, in which everyone made themselves ridiculous, the terrorist with his jargon, the parents with their nervous legalisms, the business-oriented brother and his moralizing sister. But it worked, and after a brief hesitation he allowed himself to go onstage and be applauded with the actors and the director.

Therese hadn't read the play and was uninhibited in her delight at his success. This did him good. At dinner after the premiere she kept smiling at him so warmly that despite his normal awkwardness at social events he felt his own inhibitions slip away. He realized that the director hadn't twisted his play toward travesty, but that that was how the man had understood it. Should he accept the fact that without his own knowledge or intent, he'd written a travesty?

They went back to the hotel elated. The room had been made up for the night, the curtains closed, and the bed turned down. He ordered a half bottle of champagne, they sat on the sofa in their pajamas, and he popped the cork. There was nothing more to say, but it didn't matter. There was a CD player on the chest of drawers, along with some CDs, including one with French accordion music. She snuggled up to him, and he put his arm around her shoulders. Then the CD and the champagne both came to an end. They went to bed, where after a fleeting kiss they turned with their backs to each other.

The next day they took their time on the homeward journey; they visited the art museum in Baden-Baden, stopped at a wine grower's, and went to the castle in Heidelberg. Once again it was easy to spend time together. Although the sensation of the phone in the pocket of his trousers made him feel queasy. He'd switched it off—what pile of messages might there be waiting?

2

None, as he discovered back home that evening. Anne, his girlfriend, hadn't left any word. He couldn't tell whether any calls from her were among the ones that had come in; maybe the blocked number was hers, maybe not.

He called her. He was sorry he hadn't been able to call from the hotel last night, it had been too late. He'd left early this morning, he hadn't wanted to disturb her so early. Yes, and he had forgotten his cell phone at home. "Did you try to reach me?"

"It was the first evening for weeks that we haven't talked to each other. I missed you."

"I missed you too."

It was true. Last night had felt wrong. The closeness in the shared bed had been too much. It hadn't corresponded to any inner closeness born of love or desire or even a longing for warmth or fear of loneliness. With Anne, the shared bed would have felt right, as would the night.

"When are you coming?" Her question was both tender and urgent.

"I thought you were coming." Hadn't she promised to come for a few weeks after the course she was giving at Oxford—weeks that made him both nervous and full of anticipation.

"Yes, but it's another month till then."

"I'll try to come the weekend after next."

She said nothing. When he was about to ask if there was a problem about the weekend after next, she said, "You sound different."

"Different?"

"Different from before. What's wrong?"

"Everything's fine. Maybe I partied too long after the premiere and got to bed too late and got up too early."

"What did you do all day today?"

"I did research in Heidelberg. I want to set a scene there." Nothing else occurred to him on the spur of the moment. So now he'd have to write a scene in Heidelberg in his next play.

She was silent again, before saying, "This isn't good for us. You there and me here. Why don't you write here while I'm still teaching?"

"I can't, Anne, I can't. I'm meeting the head of the Konstanz Theater and the editor of the theater publishing house, and I promised Steffen I'd help in the election. You think that unlike you, I can set things up any way I want. But I can't stop and just leave everything lying around." He was getting irritated at her.

"Election . . ."

"Nobody forced you . . ." He wanted to say that nobody had forced her to accept the teaching post in Oxford. But her field happened to be the rather narrow one of feminist legal theory, which meant that she didn't get tenure anyway, just teaching contracts. She could have broadened her field. But it was all she wanted to do, and the requests for her courses showed him that she was good at what she did. No, he didn't want to get mean. "We have to plan things better if anyone wants something from either of us. We have to work out what we're going to take on and what we're going to say no to."

"Can you come Wednesday already?"

"I'll try."

"I love you."

"I love you too."

3

He had a bad conscience. He had lied to Anne, he had got angry with her, he had almost been mean to her, and he was glad the phone conversation with her was over. When he stepped out onto the balcony and noticed the summer warmth and the peace of the city, he sat down. Sometimes a car came down the street below the balcony, sometimes the sound of footsteps echoed up to him. He also had a bad conscience because he didn't call Therese to ask if she'd survived it all and enjoyed it.

Then he was tired of having a bad conscience. He didn't owe Therese anything. What he was concealing from Anne, he had to conceal from her, because she would react with such excessive jealousy. Earlier girlfriends hadn't been troubled when they heard that he'd shared a bed with another woman while he was off on a trip or visiting someone, so long as it was only the bed. Anne would be beside herself. Why must she make such a fuss about another woman? And that she should think he wrote the rules for his own life himself and was available anytime, while she had to obey the laws of her career—how could this not make him angry? She had chosen her path just as he had chosen his.

He was glad the phone conversation was over and yet he was already living in anticipation of the next. They had known and loved each other for seven years and had still not been able to give their life together a reliable form. Anne had an apartment and a teaching contract in Amsterdam that wasn't enough to live on but that she could set aside at any time to go teach in England or America or Canada or Australia or New Zealand. He would go visit her there and stay for sometimes longer, sometimes shorter periods. Between times she was with him for days or weeks in Frankfurt, and he was with her for days or weeks in Amsterdam. In Frankfurt he found her too demanding and she found him too petty, and in Amsterdam there was less tension, either because she was more generous than he or because he was more modest in his expectations. They spent a good third of each year together. For the rest of the time Anne's life was unsettled, a life of suitcases and hotels, while his followed a peaceful track—with events and appointments, the authors' union, and the political party, with friends and, yes, Therese.

Not that any of it was so important to him. He rejoiced over every event that fell through, every appointment that got canceled, every political invitation and demand that failed to make its way to his mailbox or his e-mail. But to drag himself away from it all and move to Anne in Amsterdam or with her into the wide world—no, it was not possible.

It was not possible, although he often suffered her absence like a physical pain. When he was happy and would have liked to share that happiness with her, when he was unhappy and could have used her comfort, when he was unable to talk to her about his thoughts and his projects, when he was lying alone in bed. For all that, when they were together they didn't talk much about his thoughts and his projects, and she wasn't so sensitive when he wanted comfort nor as effusive as he would have liked when he was happy. She was a determinedly purposeful woman, and the first time he saw her, he saw this purposeful determination in her beautiful peasant face, with its many freckles and her red-blond hair, and he liked her immediately. He also liked her heavy, powerful, dependable body. Going to sleep with that body, waking up with it, finding it in bed at night—when they were together it was as wonderful as he fantasized it was when they were apart.

No matter how they longed for each other, no matter how good things were when they were together—they had destructive fights. Because he had come to terms with a life that was more separate than together and she had not. Because he wasn't as flexible and available to her as she felt he could be. Because she didn't make the compromises in her career that he felt she could. Because she spied around in his things. Because he lied, when small lies promised to bypass large conflicts. Because he could do nothing right. Because she often felt unrespected and unloved. When she got really angry she screamed at him, and he retreated into his shell. Sometimes when she was screaming he got an awkward, helpless grin on his face that only made her angrier.

But the wounds from their fights healed faster than the pains of longing. After a time all that remained of the fights was the memory that there was something there, a hot wellspring that bubbled up again and again, hissing and steaming, and that could even scald and burn them to death if they fell in. But they could avoid falling in. Perhaps one day it would even turn out that the boiling wellspring was only an apparition. One day? Perhaps even the next time they came together, with such longing and such joy!

4

He didn't fly on Wednesday, not till Friday. As he was eating dinner on Monday at the Italian restaurant around the corner, a man sat down next to him who had ordered a pizza and was waiting to pick it up. They fell into conversation, the man introduced himself as a producer, and they talked about material and plays and films. As they left, the man invited him to come have coffee in his office on Thursday. It was his first encounter with a film producer; he had been dreaming of movies for a long time, but had no one to offer his dreams to. So he changed his reservation from Wednesday to Friday.

He didn't fly to England with a contract for a treatment or a screenplay in his pocket as he'd hoped. Nonetheless the producer had invited him to write an outline for one or another of the pieces of material they'd discussed. Was that already a success? He didn't know, he was totally ignorant of the world of film. But he was in a good mood as he sat in the plane and in a good mood when he arrived.

He didn't see Anne and called her. An hour from Oxford to Heathrow, an hour at the airport, an hour to get back—she had to finish an essay and had stayed at her desk. Surely he didn't want her to have to spend the whole evening working. No, that's not what he wanted. But he thought she could have started the essay sooner. He didn't say so.

The college had provided her with a small duplex apartment. He had a key, opened the door, and went in. "Anne!" He climbed the stairs and found her at her desk. She stayed seated, wrapped her arms around his stomach, and leaned her head against his chest. "Give me another half hour. Then we go for a walk? I haven't been out of the house for the last two days."

He knew it wouldn't be a half hour, unpacked, settled in, and made notes on his conversation with the producer. When they were finally walking through the park by the Thames, the sun was already low, the sky was glowing a deep blue, the trees were throwing long shadows on the shorn grass, and the birds had stopped singing. A mysterious stillness lay over the park, as if it had fallen out of the bustle of the everyday world.

For a long time neither of them spoke. Then Anne asked, "Who were you with in Baden-Baden?"

What was she asking? The night in Baden-Baden, the phone conversation the next evening, the little lie, his bad conscience—he'd thought all that was behind him.

"With who?"

"What makes you think I . . ."

"I called Brenners Park-Hotel. I called a lot of hotels, but in Brenners they asked if they should wake their honored guests."

Which side of the bed had the telephone been on? At the thought that she might have told them to put her through, he panicked. But she hadn't told them to put her through. How did they speak in Brenners Park-Hotel? Should we wake our honored guests? "Our honored guests—they say that whether it's a question of more than one person or just one. It's an old-world form of expression that high-class hotels consider distinguished. Why didn't you ask to be put through to my room?"

"I'd had enough."

He put an arm around her. "Our verbal misunderstandings! Do you remember when I wrote to you that I wished we could smoosh up together and you thought I wanted to schmooze with you and talk all sorts of stupid gossip? Or when you said to me that in principle you'd come to our family reunion, and I thought you were saying 'basically, yes,' when all you meant was that you'd think about it?"

"Why didn't you tell me that you were in Brenners Park-Hotel? I asked them if they were full and they said yes. So you must have booked ahead. Other times you tell me where you're spending the night when you know in advance."

"I forgot. I booked weeks ago, and just got into the car on Friday and didn't look at the paper stuff with the address and the time of the performance and the reservation till I got to Baden-Baden. Because I was late getting there, all I had time to do was check in and change my clothes: I couldn't call you. After the play and the party I didn't want to call and get you out of bed."

"A four-hundred-euro room—you don't normally do that."

"Brenners is special, and a night there is something I've dreamed of for years. I . . ."

"And the fact that you made a booking for this old dream of yours is something you forgot? Why are you lying to me?"

"I'm not lying to you." He told her about the stress of the last weeks, about the various other things that had slipped his mind, even things that mattered to him and he would have liked to have done.

She was still mistrustful. "Brenners was your dream, and you get there so late and leave so early that you have no time to enjoy the hotel? It makes no sense!"

"No, it makes no sense. But then I haven't been making much sense to myself these last few weeks." He went on talking about stress and pressure, contracts and appointments, meetings and phone conferences. He talked himself into a picture of his life in the past weeks that was exaggerated but not entirely unfounded, and that Anne had no right and no cause to disbelieve. The longer he talked, the more certain he became. Wasn't it outrageous that Anne mistrusted him baselessly and unjustifiably and had doubts about him? And wasn't it laughable that she was knocking herself out about a night with a woman he hadn't had sex with and didn't even feel really close to? Knocking herself out in a park that was filled with the warmth of summer and the still of the evening and lay spell-bound under the light of the first stars?

5

Eventually the energy ran out of the argument the way a car runs out of gas. Like a car it faltered, juddered, faltered again, and came to a stop. The two of them went out to dinner and made plans. Did they have to spend the weeks when Anne could come to him in Frankfurt? Couldn't they go to Sicily or Provence or Brittany, rent a house or an apartment and write with their desks next to each other?

In the apartment they took the mattress off the worn sagging bed frame, laid it on the floor, and made love. In the middle of the night he was woken by the sound of Anne crying. He took her in his arms. "Anne," he said. "Anne."

"I have to know the truth, always. I can't live with lies. My father lied to my mother, he cheated on her and he made promise after promise to my brother and me that he never kept. When I asked him why, he got mad and yelled at me. During my entire childhood I never once had solid ground beneath my feet. You need to tell me the truth so that I've got solid ground beneath my feet. Do you understand? Do you promise?"

For a moment he thought of telling Anne the truth about the night in Brenners Park-Hotel. But what a drama that would produce! And would the truth outweigh the fact that he'd lied to Anne for a whole hour, no, two? And wouldn't a belated acknowledgment about the night with Therese give it more weight than it actually had? In the future, yes, in the future he'd tell Anne the truth. For the future he could and would promise her that. "It's all fine, Anne. I understand you. You don't have to cry. I promise I'll tell you the truth."

6

Three weeks later they drove to Provence. In Cucuron they found an old, cheap hotel on the market square where they were able to rent the big room with its big loggia on the top floor for four weeks. They wouldn't be served breakfast or dinner, and there was no Internet, and the beds were made only haphazardly. But they got a second table and a second chair and could work side by side in the room or on the loggia, just as they had pictured it.

They began assiduously. But as the days passed, work seemed less and less urgent and less and less important. Not because it was too hot; the thick walls and ceilings of the old building kept the room and the loggia cool. Work—she was writing a book on gender differences and equal rights, and he was working on a play about the financial crisis—just didn't fit. What did fit was sitting outside the Bar de l'Étang by the rectangular walled village pond, drinking an espresso and gazing into the plane trees and the water. Or driving into the mountains. Or discovering new varieties of grape at a vineyard. Or laying flowers at Camus's grave in the cemetery at Lourmarin. Or strolling through the town of Aix and catching up with e-mails in the library. The stroll would have been nicer without the e-mails, but Anne was waiting for confirmation about a job and he for a contract for a play.

"It's the light," he said. "In this light you can work in the fields or the vineyards or the olive groves, and maybe you can even write—about love and childbirth and death, but not about banks and stock exchanges."

"The light and the smells. They're so intense! The lavender and the pines and the fish and the cheese and the fruit in the market. The thoughts I put into my readers' heads—what are they compared to these smells?"

"Yes," he laughed, "but with these smells in your nose, who would want to change the world anymore? Your readers are supposed to change the world."

"Are they really?"

They were sitting on the loggia with their laptops in front of them. He looked at her, astonished. Didn't she want to change the world, and didn't she write and teach so that her students and readers would want to change it too? Wasn't that why she had refused to make compromises and tailor her career to the requirements of various universities? She was looking out over the roofs, and there were tears in her eyes. "I want a child."

He stood up, went to her, squatted down by her chair, and smiled at her. "That can be arranged."

"How would it be supposed to go? Given my life, how can I have a child?"

"You come live with me. For the first few years you stop teaching and concentrate on your writing. After that, we'll see."

"After that no university will invite me to come. They invite me because they know I'll be available. And I'm not as good a writer as I am a teacher. I've been working on my book for years."

"Universities will invite you because you're a great teacher. And so that they don't forget you in those first years, maybe it's no bad thing if you write a couple of essays instead of the book. You know, in a couple of years the world is going to look quite different again, and there will be new professional possibilities and new courses of study, and that means new jobs for you. So many things are changing so quickly."

She shrugged her shoulders. "Everything is also being forgotten so quickly."

He put his arms around her. "Yes and no. Didn't you tell me the dean at Williams invited you because the two of you were in the same seminar twenty years ago and she was so impressed by you? People don't forget you that quickly."

That evening in Bonnieux they found a restaurant with a terrace and a wide view over the countryside. The large group of Australian tourists taking up most of the tables with their joyful chatter left early, and they were alone in the darkness. Under her astonished questioning gaze, he ordered champagne.

"What are we toasting?" She twisted the glass between her thumb and forefinger.

"Our wedding!"

She kept twisting it. Then she looked at him with a sad smile. "I always knew what I wanted. I also know that I love you. Just as I know you love me. And I want children and I want to have them with you. And children and marriage go together. But today's the first time we've talked about it—give me a little time." Her smile brightened. "Shall we drink to your proposal?"

7

A few days later they went to bed in the afternoon, made love, and then went to sleep. When he woke, Anne was gone. A note told him she'd driven to Aix to check her e-mails at the library.

That was at four o'clock. By seven he was surprised she still wasn't back, and by eight he was worried. They had brought their cell phones with them on the trip, but switched them off and left them in the chest of drawers. He checked, and there they were. By nine he couldn't stand it in the room anymore and went to the village pond where they parked their car.

It was standing where it always stood. He looked around and saw Anne; she was sitting at a table outside of the dark, closed Bar de l'Étang, smoking. She'd given up smoking years ago.

He went over and stood in front of the table. "What's the matter? I was getting worried."

She didn't look up. "You were with Therese in Baden-Baden."

"What gives you . . ."

Now she looked at him. "I read your e-mails. Booking a double room. Arranging to meet Therese. Your greeting afterward: It was lovely to be with you, and I hope you survived the trip okay and everything was fine when you got home." She was crying. "It was lovely to be with you."

"You went spying in my e-mails? And do you go spying in my desk and my closet? Do you think you have the right . . ."

"You're a liar, you're a cheat, you do whatever suits you— yes, I have every right to protect myself from you. I don't get the truth from you so I have to find it myself." She was crying again. "Why did you do it? Why did you do that to me? Why did you sleep with her?"

"I didn't sleep with her."

She screamed at him. "Stop lying to me, will you just finally stop lying. You take this woman to a romantic hotel and share a room and a bed with her, and you take me for a fool? First you think I'm too dumb to see through your lies, and now you think I'm so dumb I'll let myself be talked out of the truth? You motormouth, you fucker, you piece of shit, you . . ." She was shaking with outrage.

He sat down facing her. He knew he shouldn't care if windows opened and people looked out and ridiculed them. But he did care. Being screamed at was humiliating enough; being screamed at in front of other people was a double humiliation. "May I say something?"

" 'May I say something?' " she imitated him. "The little boy is asking his mummy if he can say something? Because his mummy is always suppressing him and never allows him to say a word? Don't play the victim! Just finally take responsibility for the things you say and do! You're a liar and a cheat—at least you can admit it!"

"I'm not a . . ."

She struck him on the mouth, and seeing a revulsion in his eyes that shocked her, she kept on screaming. She leaned forward, her spit hit his face, and when he recoiled it only made her louder and more enraged. "You piece of shit, you asshole, you piece of nothing! No, you can't say something. When you talk, you lie, and I've had it with your lies, which means I've had it with your talk. Do you understand?"

"I . . ."

"Do you understand?"

"I'm sorry."

"Sorry about what? That you're a liar and a cheat? That you and other women . . ."

"I don't have other women. What I'm sorry about . . ."

"Go fuck yourself with your lies." She stood up and left.

At first he wanted to follow her, but then he stayed sitting. He suddenly remembered the trip in the car when a girlfriend revealed to him that she had other men besides him. They were driving on a winding road in Alsace, and after her admission he simply drove straight ahead off the road and onto a forest path and off the path through the bushes at a tree. Nothing happened, the car just stopped. He put his hands on the steering wheel and his head on his hands and was sad. He had no desire to attack his girlfriend. He hoped she'd be able to explain what she'd done in a way that he'd understand. That he could make his peace with. Why wouldn't Anne have it explained to her?

8

He stood up and went to the pond. It began to rain; he heard the first drops splashing gently into the water and saw the surface ripple before he felt them. Then suddenly he was wet. The rain rustled in the plane trees and on the gravel, pouring as if to wash away everything that didn't deserve to exist.

He would have liked to stand in the rain with Anne, put his arms around her from behind and feel her body under her wet clothes. Where was she? Was she outdoors too? Was she enjoying the rain the way he was, and did she understand that their stupid quarrel should just be washed away by it? Or had she ordered a taxi and was packing her clothes in the hotel?

No, when he came in, her clothes were still there. She wasn't. He took off his wet clothes and lay down. He wanted to stay awake, wait for her, talk to her. But the rain was pattering outside and the day had made him tired and the fight had left him exhausted, and he fell asleep. Sometime in the middle of the night he woke up. Anne was lying beside him. She was on her back, arms crossed behind her head, eyes wide open. He propped himself up and looked at her face. She didn't look at him. He lay down on his back too.

"The feeling that I can't contradict a woman, that I'm not allowed to refuse her anything, that I have to be alert and anticipate what she wants and flirt with her—I think it's all to do with my mother. I feel it all the time, and I behave that way automatically, whether I'm attracted to the woman or not, or whether I want anything from her or not. As a result I create expectations that I can't fulfill; for a time I try to fulfill them anyway, then it becomes too much for me and I sneak away, or the woman has enough and retreats. It's a fool's game, and I ought to learn to leave it alone. Should I talk to a therapist about me and my mother? Whatever—the game reaches its limit before it leads to sex, it doesn't even lead to preliminaries. Maybe I put an arm around the woman or squeeze her hand, but that's all. Maybe the limits have something to do with my mother too. I don't want to owe the woman anything, and if I slept with her, I'd owe her something. In my whole life I've only slept with women I loved or had at least fallen in love with. I don't love Therese, nor am I in love with her. It could be lovely with her, light somehow, undemanding, relaxed, in a way that things almost never are with us. But I've never asked myself if it was a possibility or if I wanted to leave you and live with her.

"That's one thing I wanted to say to you. The other is that . . ."

She interrupted him. "What did the two of you do the next day?"

"We went to the art museum in Baden-Baden, and a winery and the castle in Heidelberg."

"Why did you call her from here?"

"What gives you . . ." He realized that he'd started to say the same thing when she'd asked him about the trip with Therese, and that he was being interrupted the same way.

"I saw it on your phone. You called her three days ago."

"She had a biopsy because there was a suspicion of breast cancer, and I asked her how it went."

"Her breasts . . ." She said it as if she were shaking her head. "Does she know you're here with me? Does she have any idea we're together? For seven years now? What does she know about me?"

He hadn't concealed Anne from Therese, but he'd left things vague. When he went to see her, he was going to Amsterdam or London or Toronto or Wellington to write. He mentioned seeing Anne there, and didn't rule out the possibility that he was living with her there, but he also didn't make it clear. He didn't tell Therese about the difficulties he had with Anne, and told himself that that would be a betrayal. But he didn't ever talk about his happiness with Anne either. He told Therese that although he liked her a lot, he didn't love her, but he didn't tell her he loved Anne. On the other hand he hadn't kept Therese's existence from Anne either. Though he also hadn't told her how often they saw each other.

It wasn't right and he knew it, and sometimes felt like a bigamist with one family in Hamburg and the other in Munich. Like a bigamist? That was too severe. He wasn't presenting anyone with a false picture. He was presenting sketches rather than pictures, and sketches aren't false, because that's all they are—sketches. Luckily he'd told Therese that Anne was going to be in Provence too. "She knows we've been together for years and we're together here. What else she knows—I don't talk about you much to friends and acquaintances."

Anne didn't respond. He didn't know if this was a good sign or a bad one, but after a time his tension eased. He realized how tired he was. He struggled to stay awake and to hear whatever Anne might say. His eyes closed, and at first he thought he could manage to be awake even with his eyes closed, but then he realized he was falling asleep, or rather, no, that he'd already nodded off and then woken up again. What had woken him? Had Anne said something? He propped himself up again; she was lying beside him with her eyes open, but still didn't look at him. The moon was no longer shining into the room.

Then she spoke. There was the gray light of dawn outside, so he must have gone to sleep. "I don't know if I can get over what happened. But I know I won't be able to get over it if you keep trying to fool me that it was all nothing. It looks like a duck, it quacks like a duck, and you want me to believe it's a swan? I'm sick of your lies, I'm sick of them, sick of them. If I'm going to stay with you, then it's got to be the truth." She pushed back the covers and got up. "I think it's best if we don't see each other again till tonight. I'd like to have the room and Cucuron to myself. Take the car and go someplace."

9

While she was in the bathroom, he got dressed and left. The air was still cool, the streets still empty, not even the baker or the café were open yet. He got into the car and drove.

He went to the mountains of Luberon and when the road forked or came to a crossroads, he simply took whichever one promised to lead higher into the mountains. When it had nowhere further to climb, he parked the car and followed the well-worn, overgrown wheel ruts along the ridge and down the far slope.

Why didn't he just say he'd slept with Therese? What was it in him that fought so hard against this? That it wasn't true? He had had no trouble lying otherwise, when it was to avoid conflict. Why was he finding it so hard now? Because otherwise he was making the world only a little more pleasant whereas now he would be making himself look worse than he was?

He suddenly remembered how his mother, when he was a little boy and had done something he shouldn't, would give him no peace until he confessed the bad desires that had driven him to the bad deeds. Later he read about the ritual of criticism and self-criticism in the Communist Party, in which anyone who'd deviated from the party line was hammered at until he repented of his bourgeois tendencies—it was what his mother had done with him and what Anne was doing with him now. Had he sought his mother in Anne and found her again?

So, no false confessions. Break it off with Anne. Didn't they fight far too much? Wasn't he sick of her screaming at him? Sick of her spying into his laptop and his telephone and his desk and his cupboard? Sick of her expecting that when she needed him, he'd have to be there for her? Wasn't Anne's intensity too much for him? Lovely as it was to sleep with her—did it have to be so weighted with feeling and meaning? Mightn't it be lighter, more playful, more physical with someone else? And the traveling—at first there had been a certain charm to spending three or four weeks in the spring at some college in the American West and the fall at a university on the Australian coast, and in between several months in Amsterdam, but now it was actually a chore. The rolls with fresh herring you could buy from street stalls in Amsterdam were delicious. But beyond that?

He passed the foundations of a stable or a barn and sat down. How high in the mountains he was! In front of him a slope covered in olive trees tilted downward toward a flat valley, behind it were low mountains, and behind those was the plain with its little towns, one of which was Cucuron. On clear days could one see the sea from here? He heard the chirping of cicadas and the bleating of sheep, though he was unable to spot them when he looked. The sun rose higher in the sky, warming his body and releasing the scent of the rosemary.

Anne. Whatever it was that was wrong with her—when they made love in the afternoon, first in the bright daylight and then again as dusk fell, they couldn't get enough of looking at each other and touching each other, and when they lay side by side, exhausted and satisfied, talking came quite naturally. And how he loved to watch her swim, in a lake or in the sea, compact and strong and as supple as a sea otter. How he loved to watch her playing with children and dogs, oblivious of herself and the world, given over to the moment. How happy he was when she focused on a thought he'd had and lightly but surely touched on the point where he'd got carried away. How proud he was when they were together with his friends or hers and she dazzled with her mind and her wit. How safe he felt when they were holding each other.

He was reminded of a report about German, Japanese, and Italian soldiers in Russian prisoner-of-war camps. The Russians tried to indoctrinate their captives and also induct them into the ritual of criticism and self-criticism. The Germans, accustomed to leadership and robbed of it, went along with the ritual; the Japanese preferred to be killed rather than collaborate with the enemy. The Italians played along, but didn't take the proceedings seriously, cheering and clapping as if they were at the opera. Should he too play along with Anne's criticism and self-criticism session, without taking it seriously? With laughter in his heart, should he admit whatever she wanted to have admitted?

But admitting it wouldn't be the end of things. She would want to know how it could have come to that. She wouldn't rest until she'd found out what was wrong with him. Until he'd seen it too. And the insights thus won would be put to use again and again as explanations and accusations.

10

Only now did he notice how far he'd walked and how long he'd been sitting on the wall. On the way back he kept expecting at every bend of the path to find the road beyond and his car standing there, but there would be another bend and then yet another. When he finally did reach the car and looked at his watch, he saw it was noon and he was hungry.

He drove further into the mountains and found a restaurant in the next village with tables out on the street and a view of the church and the town hall. There were sandwiches, and he ordered one with ham and one with cheese and wine and water and a café au lait. The waitress was young and pretty and took her time; she calmly enjoyed his admiration and explained what kind of ham she could fetch from the butcher around the corner and what kind of cheese she had. First she brought the wine and the water, and before the sandwiches reached him he was already a little drunk.

He remained the only guest. When the carafe of wine was empty, he asked if there might be a bottle of champagne somewhere in the cellar. She laughed, gave him a pleased and conspiratorial look, and when she bent forward to clear the plates from the table, the neckline of her blouse revealed the top of her breasts. He looked after her and called, "Bring two glasses!"

She laughed. Pleased that he stood up and pulled the chair out for her. Pleased that he popped the champagne cork with a bang. Pleased that he clinked glasses with her. Pleased that he asked such careful questions about what life as an attractive woman was like in a godforsaken mountain village. In the summer she helped her grandmother in the restaurant. Otherwise she studied photography in Marseille, traveled a lot, had lived in America and Japan and published already. Her name was Renée.

"I close up between three and five."

"Do you take a midday nap?"

"It would be the first time."

"What could be nicer at midday than . . ."

"I know what could be nicer." She laughed.

She looked at the time. "Today I'm closing the restaurant at two thirty already."

"Good."

They stood up and took the champagne with them. He followed her through the dining room and the kitchen. His head was swimming from the champagne and the prospect of sex, and as Renée climbed the dark staircase in front of him, he could have ripped the clothes from her body right then and there—but he had the bottle and the glasses in his hands. At that moment Anne and her quarrel went through his head—wasn't there a principle that if one is condemned for an act one has not in fact committed, one cannot then be punished as and when one actually commits it? Double jeopardy? Anne had punished him for something he hadn't done. So now he was allowed to do it.

Renée laughed a lot in bed too. She laughed as she took out the bloody tampon and set it on the floor next to the bed. She made love as functionally and skillfully as if she were playing a sport. Only after they were both exhausted did she become tender and wanted to kiss him and be kissed by him. The second time she held him tighter than she had the first, but afterward she soon checked the time and sent him away. It was four thirty. Her grandmother would be back soon. And he wasn't to come back; in three days her time in, what had he called it, her godforsaken village in the mountains, would be over.

She accompanied him to the staircase. From downstairs he looked up one more time: she was leaning against the banisters, and in the darkness he couldn't read the expression on her face.

"It was lovely with you."

"Yes."

"I like your laugh."

"Get going."

11

He would have liked a summer storm, but the sky was blue and the heat hung in the narrow street. As he got into the car he saw a Mercedes pull up outside the restaurant and an old couple get out. Renée came through the door, greeted them both, and helped them carry groceries into the house.

He drove slowly in order to keep Renée in his rearview mirror for a little. He was suddenly overwhelmed with a powerful longing for another life, a life with winter in the city by the sea and summer in the village in the mountains, a life with its own unchanging, reliable rhythm, in which one always drove the same routes, slept in the same bed, met the same people.

He wanted to walk in the same place he'd walked that morning, but didn't find the spot. He stopped at another one, got out, couldn't decide about walking again, but sat among the bushes, plucked a blade of grass, propped his arms on his knees, and put the grass between his teeth. Again he was looking out over slopes and low mountains into the plain. His longing wasn't swirling around Renée or around Anne. It wasn't about this woman or that, but about continuity and reliability in life itself.

He fantasized about giving them all up, Renée, who didn't want him anyway; Therese, who only liked the bits of him that were simple; Anne, who wanted to be conquered but not to conquer herself. But then he'd have nobody left.

He'd tell Anne that evening what she wanted to hear. Why not? Yes, she'd always take what he said and make use of it later. But so what? What harm could it do him? What harm could anything do him? He felt invulnerable, untouchable, and laughed—it must be the champagne.

It was too early to drive back to Cucuron and Anne. He stayed sitting and looked down at the plain. Sometimes a car passed, sometimes it honked. Sometimes he saw something flash down on the plain—the sunlight catching the window in a house or the windshield of a car.

He dreamed about summer in the village in the mountains. He and Renée or Chantal or Marie or whatever she would be called would move up there in May and open up the restaurant, not for lunch but just for guests in the evening, two or three dishes, simple country cooking, local wines. A few tourists would come, a few foreign artists who'd bought old houses and renovated them, a few locals. Early in the morning he'd drive to the market for supplies, early in the afternoon they'd make love, in the late afternoon they'd go to the kitchen together and prepare the food. Mondays and Tuesdays they'd be closed. In October they'd close the restaurant, lock the shutters and the door, and drive back to the city. A gallery or a bookshop? Stationery? Tobacco? A shop just open in winter? How would that work? Did he even want to run a shop? Operate a restaurant? They were all empty dreams. Love in the early afternoon was what counted, no matter whether it was in a town by the sea or a river or in a village in the mountains or on the plain.

He looked down at the plain and chewed his blade of grass.

12

He reached Cucuron at seven, parked the car, didn't find Anne outside the Bar de l'Étang, and went into the hotel. She was sitting in the loggia, a bottle of red wine on the table and two glasses, one full and one empty. How was she looking at him? He really didn't want to know. He looked at the floor.

"I don't want to say much. I slept with Therese and I'm sorry and I hope you can forgive me and we can put it behind us, not today, I know, and not tomorrow, but soon, so that we can stay good to each other. I love you, Anne, and . . ."

"Won't you sit down?"

He sat down, went on talking and kept looking at the floor. "I love you, and I don't want to lose you. I hope I haven't already lost you because of something so insignificant. I understand that it's really significant to you, and because of that and because I should have known it, it should have been significant for me too and I shouldn't have done it. I understand that. But it really is insignificant. I know that . . ."

"Settle down. Do you want . . ."

"No, Anne, please let me say it all. I know men keep saying, and women say it too, that a little infidelity is meaningless, that it just happens, that it's a fleeting opportunity, or loneliness, or alcohol, that it leaves nothing behind, no demands. They say it so often that it's become a cliché. But clichés are clichés because they're true, and even though infidelity is sometimes something different—often it is nothing, and that's how it was with me. Therese and I in Baden-Baden—it was meaningless. You may . . ."

"Can you . . ."

"In a moment you can say whatever you want to say. I only want to say that I understand if you don't want someone to whom a little infidelity means nothing. But the part of me to which a little infidelity means nothing is only a small part of me. The larger part of me is the one to which you mean more than anyone in the world, which loves you, with which you have been together for years. And before Baden-Baden I never . . ."

"Look at me!"

He looked up and looked at her.

"It's fine. I called Therese and she confirmed that nothing happened. Perhaps you want to know why I didn't believe you and yet I believe her—I can tell better from a woman's voice whether she's telling the truth or lying than I can from a man's. She felt you weren't honest with her or with me, and if she'd known how long you and I had been together and how close we were, she wouldn't have wanted to see you so often. But that's another story. In any case, you didn't sleep together."

"Oh!" He didn't know what to say. In Anne's face he saw hurt, relief, and love. He ought to get to his feet, go to her, and hug her. But he stayed sitting down and just said, "Come here!" and she stood up and came to sit on his lap and lean her head against his shoulder. He put his arms around her and looked out over her head at the rooftops and the church tower. Should he tell her about his afternoon with Renée?

"Why are you shaking your head?"

Because I've just decided not to tell you about the other little infidelity this afternoon . . . "I was just thinking that we almost . . ."

"I know."

13

They didn't say any more about Baden-Baden, or Therese, or truth and lies. It wasn't as if nothing had taken place. If nothing had taken place, they would have felt free to fight with each other. But they were taking care not to bang into each other. They moved cautiously. They did more work than they had at the beginning and by the end she had completed her essay on gender differences and equal rights, and he had his play about two bankers sitting trapped in an elevator for a whole weekend. When they had sex, each of them remained a little reserved.

On the last evening they went again to the restaurant in Bonnieux. They watched from the terrace as the sun went down and night came. The deep blue of the sky darkened to absolute black, the stars glittered, and the cicadas were loud. The blackness, the glitter, the noise—it was a festive night. But their imminent departure made them melancholic, and on top of this the star-strewn sky reminded him of moral law and the hour with Renée.

"Are you still holding it against me that I didn't tell Therese more about you and you more about Therese?"

She shook her head. "It made me sad. But I don't hold it against you. And you? Do you hold it against me that I suspected you and used blackmail? Which is what I did, I blackmailed you, and because you love me, you allowed it to happen."

"No, I don't hold it against you. It makes me anxious that things escalated so fast. But that's something else."

She laid her hand on his, but instead of looking at him, she looked out across the countryside. "Why are we this way? . . . I don't know what to call it. You know what I mean? We've changed."

"Changed for the better or for the worse?"

She took her hand out of his, leaned back, and looked at him sharply. "I don't know that either. We've lost something and we've won something, haven't we?"

"Lost our innocence? Won some kind of sobriety?"

"And if sobriety is also the death of love, and without some faith, pure and simple, in the other person, things can't go on?"

"Isn't truth, which you said you need as the ground beneath your feet, always sober?"

"No, the truth I mean and the one I need isn't sober. It's passionate, beautiful sometimes, and sometimes hideous, it can make you happy and it can torture you, and it always sets you free. If you don't notice it at first, you will after a while." She nodded. "It can really torture you. Then you curse and wish you'd never encountered it. But then you realize it's not torturing you, what's doing the torturing is whatever the truth is about."

"I don't understand." The truth and whatever the truth is about—what did Anne mean? At the same time he was wondering if he should tell her about Renée, now, because later would be too late. But why would later be too late? And if later was okay, why have to do it at all?

"Forget it."

"But I really want to know what . . ."

"Forget it. I'd rather talk about how things are meant to go from here."

"You wanted some time to think about getting married."

"Yes, I think I should take some time. Don't you need time too?"

"Time out?"

"Time out."

14

She didn't want to talk about it. No, he hadn't done anything wrong. Nothing she could name. Nothing she would want to talk about between the two of them and a couples therapist.

The food came. She ate enthusiastically. He felt queasy, and poked around the dorade with his fork. When they were lying in bed, she didn't push him away but she wasn't hungry for him either, and he had the feeling she didn't need time anymore, she'd already reached a decision and he had already lost her.

The next morning she asked if he'd mind taking her to the airport in Marseille. He did mind, but he took her and tried to say goodbye to her in such a way that she'd see his pain as well as his readiness to respect her decision, and would remember him fondly and would want to see him again and have him too.

Then he drove through Marseille, hoping he'd suddenly see Renée on the sidewalk, but knew he wouldn't stop. On the highway he thought about how life in Frankfurt would be without Therese. What he would work on. The contract for a new play that he'd been hoping for hadn't come. He could set to work on the outline for the movie producer—but he could do that anywhere. Nothing, in fact, was pulling him toward Frankfurt.

What had Anne said? If you encounter the truth and it tortures you, that isn't what's torturing you, it's whatever the truth's about. And it always sets you free. He laughed. Truth and whatever the truth is about—he still didn't understand. And that the truth sets you free—maybe it was the other way around and you had to be free in order to be able to live with the truth. But nothing spoke against trying out the truth anymore. Somewhere up ahead he'd leave the highway and take a room in a hotel, in the Cévennes, in Burgundy, in the Vosges, and write about it all to Anne.

The House in the Forest

1

Sometimes it felt as if this had always been his life. That he'd always lived in this house in the forest, by the meadow with its apple trees and lilacs, and the pond with its weeping willows. That he'd always had his wife and daughter around him. And always received their farewells when he went away, and their happy greetings when he came back.

Once a week they stood in front of the house and waved goodbye to him until his car was out of sight. He drove to the little town, collected the mail, took things to be repaired, collected whatever had been repaired or ordered, visited the physical therapist to do exercises for his back, and shopped at the general store. Once there he would stand for a while at the counter before the drive home, drinking a coffee, talking to a neighbor, or reading the *New York Times*. He was never away for more than five hours. He missed the company of his wife. And he missed the company of his daughter, whom he didn't take along, because she got carsick.

They heard him from a long way away. No other car took the narrow, rutted road that led to their house through a long, forested valley. They would stand in front of the house again, hand in hand, until he made the turn toward the meadow, Rita tore herself free of Kate and began to run, and flew into his arms almost before he had time to switch off the engine and get out of the car. "Papa, Papa!" He held her, overwhelmed by her tenderness as she wrapped her arms around his neck and nestled her face against his.

On those days Kate belonged to him and Rita. Together they unloaded whatever he had brought from town, did things in the house or the garden, collected wood in the forest, caught fish in the pond, pickled cucumbers or onions, baked bread. Rita, full of family happiness and exuberance, ran from her father to her mother and from her mother to her father and just talked and talked. After supper the three of them would play, or he and Kate together would tell Rita a story that they'd worked out while they were cooking.

On other days Kate disappeared in the morning from the bedroom to her study. When he brought her coffee and fruit for breakfast, she would look up from her computer with a friendly smile, and if he had a problem to discuss with her she made an effort to understand it. But her thoughts were elsewhere, as they were when the three of them sat around the table at lunch or supper. Even after Rita's good-night story and good-night kiss, when she came to sit with him and they listened to music or watched a movie or read books, her thoughts were with the characters she was writing about.

He didn't let it weigh on him. He was happy—just knowing she was in the house, seeing her head at the window while he was working in the garden, then hearing her fingers typing on the computer keyboard while he was standing at the door, having her opposite him at supper and beside him in the evening. Feeling her, smelling her, hearing her breathing in the night. And he could not expect any more of her. She had told him she could live only if she was writing, and he had told her he accepted that.

Just as he accepted that he was alone with Rita day in, day

out. He woke her, washed and dressed her, had breakfast with her, and let her watch and help with the cooking, the washing and cleaning, the gardening, the repairing of the roof and the heating and the car. He answered her questions. He taught her to read, far too soon. He romped around with her even though his back hurt, because he knew she ought to romp around.

He accepted the way things were. But he wished they were together more as a family. He wished the days with Kate and Rita were not a part of life only once a week, but yesterday, today, and tomorrow too.

Does all happiness yearn to be eternal? Like all desire? No, he thought, what it yearns for is continuity. It yearns to endure in the future, having already been happiness in the past. Don't lovers fantasize that they already met as children and were drawn to each other? That they played in the same playground or went to the same school or spent their holidays in the same place with their parents? He didn't fantasize about any early encounters. He dreamed that Kate and Rita and he had put down roots here in defiance of every wind and every storm. Forever and ever.

2

They had moved here six months ago. He had started his search for a house in the country in the spring of the previous year and had looked all summer long. Kate was too busy even to look at pictures of houses on the Internet. She said she wanted a house somewhere near New York. But didn't she want to get away from the demands that were made on her in New York? That kept her from her writing and her family? That she would love to have declined, but could not, because part of life as a famous writer in New York required being reachable and available?

He found the house with its meadows and its pond in fall: five hours from New York, on the border with Vermont, away from large towns, away from large roads, sitting enchanted in the forest. He went up there alone a couple of times to deal with the broker and the owner. Then Kate came with him.

She had been through some stressful days, went to sleep as they drove up the highway, and didn't wake up till they exited onto the country road. The sunroof was open, and above her Kate saw blue sky and brightly colored leaves. She smiled at her husband. "Drunk on sleep, drunk on colors, drunk on freedom—I don't know where I am and where we're going. I've forgotten where I've come from." The last hour of their journey took them through the glowing landscape of an Indian summer, first along country roads with a yellow line down the middle, then on rural roads with none, and finally on the dirt road that led to the house. When she got out of the car and looked around, he knew that she liked the house. Her eyes swept over the forest, the meadow, the pond, came to rest on the house, and paused on one detail after the other: the door under the front porch held up by two slender columns, the windows, aligned neither with those above them nor with those beside them, the leaning chimney, the open veranda, the addition. More than two hundred years old, despite the ravages of time the house had not lost its dignity. Kate nudged him and signaled with her eyes at the corner windows on the second floor, two of them facing the pond and one of them facing the meadow. "Is that . . . ?"

"Yes, that's your room."

The cellar was dry, the floors were sound. Before the first snows new shingles were put on and new heating installed so the tiling guy and the electrician, the carpenter and the painter, could work even in the winter. When they moved in in the spring the floors hadn't yet been polished, the open fireplace not yet bricked in, the kitchen cupboards not yet hung. But the very day after the move he led Kate into her completed study. After all their things had been unloaded and the truck had driven away, he had polished the floorboards that same evening and the next morning had brought her desk and bookshelves upstairs. She sat down at the desk, stroked the top of it, pulled open the drawer and closed it again, looked through the left-hand window at the pond and through the right-hand window at the meadow. "You positioned the desk just right—I don't want to decide between the water and the land. So when I look straight ahead, I'll be looking at the corner. In old houses ghosts come out of the corners, not through the doors."

Kate's study was next to their bedroom and Rita's bedroom; in the rear of the house was the bathroom and a little room that just held a table and chair. On the first floor, the front door opened immediately into the one large space, with its open fireplace and wooden beams, that encompassed both kitchen area, eating area, and living room.

"Shouldn't you and Rita swap? She's only in her room to sleep, and the little room is far too small for you to write in." He told himself Kate meant well. Perhaps she had a guilty conscience because in the time they had known each other, her writing career had soared while his declined. His first novel, a best seller in Germany, had found a publisher in New York and a producer in Hollywood. That was how he had met Kate, as a young German author on a reading tour in America, not a success here but full of promise and already planning his next novel. But with all the waiting for the film, which never got made, with all the traveling with Kate, who was soon being invited everywhere in the world, and with all his concerns for Rita, he'd done no more than make notes for his next novel. When asked what he did, he still said he was a writer. But he wasn't working on anything, no matter what he said to Kate and what he even pretended to himself sometimes. So what would he do in a bigger room? Feel even more strongly that he was just marking time?

He put off the next novel till later. If it still interested him. What occupied his mind more than anything was whether Rita should start kindergarten. When she did, she'd no longer belong to him.

3

Naturally both parents loved Rita. But Kate could have pictured a life without children; he couldn't. When she got pregnant, she behaved as if it were nothing. He insisted that she go to the doctor and a prenatal gymnastics class. He put the ultrasound pictures up on the bulletin board. He stroked her swollen stomach, talked to it, read it poems, and played music to it, tolerated by an amused Kate.

Kate's love was matter-of-fact. Her father, a professor of history at Harvard, and her mother, a pianist who frequently toured, had raised their four children with the kind of efficiency associated with a business. The children had a good nanny, went to good schools, got good instruction in languages and music, and were supported by their parents in everything that came into their heads. They entered life in the knowledge that they would achieve what they wanted to achieve, their husbands or wives would function well in their jobs, in their homes, and in bed, and their children would of course run just as smoothly as they had run themselves. Love was the grease that lubricated this family machine.

For him love and family were the fulfillment of a dream he

had begun to dream when the marriage of his parents, father an administrative employee, mother a bus driver, sank into a morass of spite, screaming matches, and violence. His parents hit him too sometimes. But when that happened, he accepted it as their reaction to some stupid thing he'd done. When his parents began to scream and then came to blows, he and his sisters felt as if the ice were cracking beneath their feet. His dream of love and family was thick ice, solid enough to walk on, solid enough even to dance on. At the same time the bond of love and family was as tight in his dream as the bond between him and his sisters, holding tight to one another when the storm broke.

Kate was the promise of thick ice. At a dinner at the Monterey book festival, the host had sat them next to each other: the young American author whose first novel had just been sold to Germany and the young German author who'd just arrived in America with his first novel. *If I can make it there, I'll make it anywhere*—ever since seeing his book in the bookstores in New York, he felt wonderful and he told his dinner companion enthusiastic stories about his successes and his plans. He was as clumsy as a little puppy. She was amused and moved and gave him a sense of security. He knew and hated that older, successful women felt drawn to him and wanted to look after him. Kate took care of him and was neither quite as old as he was nor quite so successful. People's opinions didn't seem to bother her. When, disconcerting his host, he suddenly stood up and invited her to dance, she laughed and accepted.

He fell in love with her that very evening. She went to sleep confused. When they met again at the book festival in Paso Robles and Kate took him to her room, he wasn't the awkward boy she had imagined, but a man of passionate abandon. No one had ever made love to her like that. Nor had anyone ever curled against her, holding so tight, when he was asleep. It was an unrestrained, all-consuming kind of love. That was unknown to her, and both frightened and aroused her. When they were back in New York, he stayed and courted her with clumsy determination till she let him move in with her. Her apartment was big enough. Because living together went well, they got married six months later.

Living together changed. At the beginning they worked with their desks together, whether at home or in the library, and they did appearances together. Then came Kate's second book, and it was a best seller. Now she did appearances alone. After her third book she went on a world tour. He often went with her, but no longer enjoyed attending the official events. Admittedly Kate always introduced him as the well-known German writer, but no one knew his name or his book and he hated people's politeness when they met him just because he was Kate's husband. He sensed her anxiety that he was jealous of her success. "I'm not jealous. You've earned your success and I love your books."

Their lives intersected less often. "It can't go on like this," he said, "you're away too much and when you're here you're too exhausted—too exhausted to talk, let alone make love."

"I find all the rushing around hard too. I'm turning almost everything down. What should I do? I can't turn it all down."

"How will it go when there's the baby?"

"Baby?"

"I found the test with the two red strips."

"That doesn't mean anything."

Kate didn't want to believe the first pregnancy test, and did a second one. When she became a mother, she also didn't want to believe at first that she would have to change her life, and lived the way she had before the baby. But when she came home in the evenings and picked up her daughter, Rita turned in her arms and reached for her father. Then Kate would be overwhelmed with longing for another life, a life with child and husband and writing and nothing else. In the bustle of the following day the longing would dissipate. But as Rita grew older, it returned all the more strongly and each time it did so, Kate was more jolted.

One evening before he went to sleep he said, "I don't want to go on living like this."

Suddenly she was afraid she would lose him and Rita, and life with the two of them seemed to her the most precious thing there was. "Nor I. I'm sick of the traveling and the readings and the lectures and the receptions. I just want to be with you both and write, that's it."

"Is that true?"

"If I can write, all I need is you two. The rest of it I don't need at all."

They tried to live a different way. After a year they knew it would never succeed in New York. "Life here eats you whole. You love meadows and trees and birds—I'll find us a house in the country."

4

After they'd lived in the country for a few months, he said, "It isn't just meadows and trees and birds. Look how everything is coming along and growing—the house is almost finished, Rita is healthier than she was in the city, and the apple trees that Jonathan and I pruned are going to produce a good crop."

They were standing in the garden. He put his arm around Kate and she leaned against him. "The only thing that isn't almost finished is my book. It'll be winter or next spring."

"That's soon! And doesn't your writing go easier than in the city?"

"I'll have a first draft in the fall. Do you want to read it?"

She had always claimed that you mustn't show anyone what you're writing or talk to anyone about it—it brings bad luck. He was pleased that she trusted him. He was pleased by the prospect of the apple crop and the fresh cider he would press. He had ordered a big vat.

Fall came early, and the early frost tinted the maples a flaming scarlet. Rita couldn't get enough of the colors of the trees or of how on cool evenings paper and logs in the fireplace could make a warming fire. He let her scrunch up the paper herself, and stack the kindling and logs, and strike the match and hold it close. But she still said, "Look, Papa, look!" It remained a miracle to her.

When the three of them sat by the fire, he served hot cider with a sprig of green mint for Rita and a shot of Calvados for Kate and him. Maybe it was because of the Calvados that she responded more often to his wooing in bed. Maybe it was because of her relief at having finished the first draft.

He wanted to read a little every day, and explained to Rita that every day she must play by herself for a little while. The first day she knocked proudly on his door after two hours, accepted his praise, and promised to spend even longer alone the next day. But by the next day he had finished. He had got out of bed in the night and read to the end.

Kate's first three novels had depicted the life of a family at the time of the Vietnam War, the eventual return of the son from captivity to the love of his life, who had married and had a daughter, and the fate of this daughter whose father was not the man her mother was married to and with whom she had grown up but the returning soldier. Each novel was self-contained, but taken together they formed the portrait of an era.

Kate's new novel was set in the present. A young couple, both successful professionals who can't have children, wants to adopt and goes searching abroad. They go from one complication to the next, are faced with medical, bureaucratic, and political hurdles, encounter committed helpers and corrupt agencies, and find themselves in comic and dangerous situations. In Bolivia, faced with the choice between adopting an enchanting pair of twins or exposing the criminals behind the arrangement and putting the adoption at risk, the man and the woman quarrel. The images they have of themselves and other people, their love, their marriage—none of it holds true anymore. In the end the adoption founders and the future they imagined for themselves lies shattered. But their lives are open to something new.

It was still dark as he laid the last page on the stack of those he'd read. He switched off the light and opened the window, breathed the cool air, and saw the hoarfrost on the meadow. He liked the book. It was gripping, moving, and written with a lightness that was new for Kate. Readers would love the book; they would share in all the hopes and emotions and enjoy thinking their own thoughts about the open ending.

But had Kate given him the manuscript because she trusted him? The couple whose lives are open to something new—was that meant to be Kate and him? Did she want to warn him? Did she want to say to him that their old life no longer worked and challenge him to embark on a new one? He shook his head and sighed. Please, not that. But perhaps it was all quite different. Perhaps she was using the end of the book to celebrate the two of them having started their own new life together. They weren't the couple with their life smashed to pieces. They were the couple whose life had been in pieces and had already embarked on their new one.

He heard the first birds. Then it got light; the dark mass of the forest behind the meadow transformed itself into individual trees. The sky wasn't yet revealing whether it would be a sunny or a cloudy day. Should he talk to Kate? Ask her if the manuscript contained a message for him? She would frown and look at him with irritation. He would have to make his own sense of the end of the young couple's search. Was a conflict smoldering beneath the life he and Kate were leading together? Kate was under stress. But how could she not be! She had wanted to stick to the deadline she had set herself for the first draft, and in the last weeks had been writing far into the night.

No, there was no conflict smoldering under their life. Since the stupid fight over the Paris Book Fair, which Kate had agreed to attend without talking to him first, but had finally canceled, they hadn't quarreled. He wasn't jealous of her success. They loved their daughter. When the three of them were together, they laughed a lot and often sang. They wanted to get a black Labrador and had registered with a breeder for one from the next litter.

He stood up and stretched. He could still sleep for an hour. He undressed and climbed the creaking stairs cautiously. Entering the bedroom on tiptoe, he paused until Kate, who'd been disturbed by the opening and closing of the door, sank back into peaceful sleep. Then he slid under the covers beside her and cuddled up close. No, no conflict.

5

On his next trip to the little town he did shopping for the winter. It really wasn't necessary; last winter it had never taken more than a day for the road to be plowed out. But the potatoes in their sack, the onions in the crate, the cabbages in the barrel, and the apples on the racks would make the cellar a cozy place for Rita. She would love climbing down there to count potatoes and bring them up.

At the farm along his route, he ordered potatoes, and onions, and cabbages. The farmer asked, "Can you take my daughter to town with you and drop her off again on the way back? When you collect your order?" So he took the sixteen-year-old daughter along who wanted to pick up some books at the library and peppered this new neighbor with curious questions. Had he and his wife had enough of the city? Were they looking for peace in the country? What had they been doing in the city? She didn't let up until she found out that he and his wife were writers, and she thought that was exciting. "What's your wife's name? Can I read something she's written?" He evaded the question.

Then he got angry. Why hadn't he said his wife was a translator or a Web designer? They hadn't fled New York in order to land up in the country in the middle of the next fuss about Kate. Then in the *New York Times* he learned that the American Book Prize was due to be awarded in the next few days. Each of Kate's books had been under consideration. This year she didn't have a new one out. But it was only this year that the critics had recognized and hailed the three novels as the portrait of an era. He couldn't imagine Kate not being in the running. If she won, the whole thing would start up again.

He drove to the library and honked. The daughter was standing in front of the entrance with some other girls; she waved, and the others looked. On the way back she told him how exciting her friends thought it was that his wife and he were writers and lived close by. Would he or his wife come to their school sometime and talk to them about writing? They'd already had a doctor and an architect and an actress come visit. "No," he said, more brusquely than was called for, "we don't do that kind of thing."

When he'd delivered her and loaded up his stuff and was alone in the car again, he drove to the scenic outlook that he'd always driven past before and stopped in the empty parking lot. In front of him the forest in all its flaming colors dipped down to a broad valley, climbed again on the far side, and glowed all the way to the first range of mountains. On the second range the colors were already faded and far in the distance from the forest, and the mountains blurred into the pale blue sky. A hawk was circling above the valley.

The farmer, who had an interest in local history, had once told him about the surprise onset of winter in 1876 and the snow that fell in the midst of Indian summer, light at first and the delight of the children, then thicker and thicker until it blanketed everything and the roads were impassable and the houses cut off. Travelers caught by the snow had no chance, but even some of those trapped inside their houses froze to death. There were some houses far from the roads from which the inhabitants didn't make it back to the villages until spring.

He looked up at the sky. Oh, if only it would snow now! Lightly at first so that whoever was out in it would get home, then so heavily that driving would be impossible for days. So that a branch would break under it and tear down the new phone line. So that no one could tell Kate she'd won and invite her to the awards ceremony, and no one could pull her into the city to burden her with interviews, talk shows, and receptions. When the thaw came, the prize would find its way to Kate, and she would be no less delighted than she would be now. But the hubbub would have come and gone, and her world would remain unchanged.

When the sun had gone down he drove on, from the main road to the local road and then the dirt road up the long valley, until he stopped and got out. New, pale, unseasoned poles ran along the roadside carrying the phone line ten feet in the air. Some trees had been felled to make room and some branches cut back. But others stood close to the line.

He found a pine with bare branches, tall, leaning, dead. He threw the work rope around the tree and hitched it to the tow bar, put the car into four-wheel drive, and then into gear. The engine howled and died. He put it into gear again, and again the engine howled and died. On the third try the wheels lost traction. He got out, took the folding spade from the emergency kit, and dug into the cracks in a rock in which the roots had taken hold. He tried to loosen them, grubbed at them, shook them, and pulled. His shirt, his sweater, his pants—everything was soaked with sweat. If only he could see better! It was getting dark.

He got back in the car, put it in gear, and eased forward until the rope was taut, let the car roll back, then accelerated again. Forward, backward, forward, backward—sweat poured down into his eyes to join the tears of rage at the tree that wouldn't fall and the world that refused to leave him and Kate in peace. He drove forward, back, forward, back. He hoped Kate and Rita couldn't hear him. He hoped Kate didn't call the farmer or the general store. He had never come home this late. He hoped she didn't call anyone else.

Without the tree giving any signal by beginning to tip, it fell. It struck the line right next to one of the poles, and both tree and pole bowed forward until the lines tore loose. Then they crashed to the ground.

He switched off the engine. Everything was silent. He was exhausted, drained, empty. But then he began to be filled with a sense of triumph. He'd done it. He would do the rest of it too. What strength he had! What strength!

He got out of the car, untied the rope, loaded it and the spade, and drove home. From far off he could see the lighted windows—his house. His wife and daughter were standing out in front as they always did, and as always Rita flew into his arms. Everything was good.

6

It was the following evening before Kate asked him why the phone and the Internet weren't working. In the mornings and early afternoons she allowed nothing to interfere with her writing, and didn't pay attention to her e-mails until late afternoon.

"I'll take a look." He stood up, went to check the boxes and wires for the phone and computer, and found nothing. "I can drive into town tomorrow and arrange for the technician to come."

"Then I'll lose another half a day—why don't you wait? Sometimes the technical stuff straightens out by itself."

After the technical stuff still hadn't straightened itself out several days later, Kate pressed him: "And if you go tomorrow, ask if there's a cell phone network we can access here. We can't cope without a cell phone."

They had both been delighted to find that there was no cell phone reception either in the house or on the property. That they weren't reachable and available at all times. That from time to time they didn't pick up the landline either, and had no answering machine. That they didn't have the mail delivered, but went to collect it. And now Kate wanted a cell phone?

They lay in bed together and Kate switched off the light. He switched it on. "Do you really want it to be like it was in New York again?" When she said nothing, he didn't know whether she hadn't understood his question or didn't want to answer it. "I mean . . ."

"Sex was better in New York than here. We were hungrier for each other. Here . . . we're like an old couple, we're tender but not passionate. As if we'd lost what passion was."

He got angry. Yes, sex was more peaceful now, more peaceful and more profound. In New York they'd often fallen onto each other in their haste and their appetite, which had had its own charm, just as life in the city was full of haste and appetite. Their sex resembled their lives, both here and back there, and if Kate was longing for haste and appetite, then it wasn't just about sex. Had she needed peace only to get her book written? Now that the book was done, was she done with life in the country too? He was no longer angry, he was afraid. "I would love to sleep with you more often. I would love to burst into your room and take you in my arms, and you'd put your arms round my neck and I'd carry you to bed. I . . ."

"I know. I didn't mean what I said. When the book's finished, it'll get better again. Don't worry."

Kate came into his arms and they made love. When he woke up next morning she was already awake and she was looking at him. She said nothing, and he turned on his side too and looked at her silently. He couldn't tell from her eyes what she was feeling or thinking, and tried not to let his look betray his anxiety. He hadn't believed her yesterday when she'd said she didn't mean it, and he didn't believe it today either. His anxiety was filled with longing and need. Her face with its high forehead, the proud arch of its eyebrows over the dark eyes, long nose, generous mouth and chin, that, smooth, or clenched, or furrowed, declared the mood Kate was in—it was the landscape inhabited by his love. That love was happily at home when her face was open and turned toward him, worried when it was closed and turned away. A face, he thought, nothing more, yet it encompasses the entire range of what I need and what I can bear. He smiled. She kept looking at him silently and seriously, but then put her arm around his back and pulled him to her.

7

On the trip to town he stopped by the fallen tree and pole and the ripped wires. As they spun, his tires had left marks on the road. He wiped them away.

It all looked as if something had simply happened. He could drive to town and alert the phone company. There was nothing yet to reproach him for. But even if he didn't report it to the phone company, there was nothing to reproach him for. He hadn't seen the fallen tree and pole and the torn wires. Why should he have seen them? It was up to the technician who had laid the wires in their house and installed the computer, and whom he had promised to notify, to notice what had happened on his way to them. Or not.

The technician wasn't in his workshop. On the door was a piece of paper saying he was visiting a customer and would be back soon. But the paper was yellowed and the filthy windows made it impossible to see whether the workshop was in use, or closed for a vacation or for the winter. Phones and computers stood on the tables, along with cables, plugs, and screwdrivers.

In the general store he was the only customer. The owner started talking to him and told him about the town fair on the upcoming Saturday. Would he like to come? And bring his wife and daughter? He had never been in the general store with Kate and Rita, nor in any shop or restaurant. They had sometimes driven through town, that was all. What else did the owner know about them?

Then he saw Kate's photo in the *New York Times*. She had won the Book Prize. She hadn't appeared for the ceremony, her agent had accepted it on her behalf, and Kate hadn't been reachable for a quote.

Didn't the owner read the paper? Had he not recognized Kate in the photo? Hadn't he seen her properly as they drove through town? Had other people seen Kate more clearly as they drove through town and recognized her in the photo? Would they call the *New York Times* and tell them where Kate could be reached? Or would they tell the *Weekly Herald,* which carried little news items alongside the ads, on crimes and accidents, openings and baptisms, jubilees, weddings, births and deaths?

Three copies of the *New York Times* were still lying next to the counter. He would have liked to buy all three, so that nobody else could buy them and read them. But that would have attracted the attention of the owner. So he bought only one. Along with it he bought a small bottle of whiskey, which the owner put in a brown paper bag for him. On the way to the car he went past stacks of blue sawhorses and police barricades that would be used to block off the main street for the fair. He drove back to the technician's workshop and again found no one there. He could say he'd tried.

He didn't even look at the mail when he took it out of the mailbox. He stuck it in the torn cover of the sun visor. He drove to the scenic viewpoint again, parked, and drank. The whiskey burned in his mouth and throat, he swallowed the wrong way and belched. He looked at the brown paper bag with the bottle in his hand and thought of the tramps sitting on the benches in Central Park with their brown paper bags, drinking. Because they hadn't been able to hold their worlds together.

The last time he had sat here, the forest had still been a blaze of color. Today the colors had dulled, consumed by the fall and dampened by the haze. He rolled down the window and inhaled the cool fresh air. He had been so looking forward to winter, the first winter in the new house, to evenings by the fire, doing handcrafts and baking together, making Advent wreaths, the Christmas tree, roasting apples, mulling wine. To Kate, who would have more time for Rita and him.

And also to their New York friends, whom they finally wanted to invite once winter came. Their real friends, Peter and Liz and Steve and Susan, not the rabble of agents and publishing and media people. Peter and Liz wrote, Steve was a teacher, and Susan made jewelry—they were the only ones he and Kate had talked to seriously about the reasons for their moving to the country. They were also the only ones to whom they had given their new address.

Yes, they had their new address. What if they came? Because they'd read the *New York Times* and concluded that the good news hadn't yet reached Kate and because they wanted to be the bearers of it?

He took another swallow. He mustn't get drunk. He must keep a clear head and think about what he should do. Call their friends? Tell them that Kate knew about the award but hadn't wanted to get involved in all the fuss? Their friends knew Kate, knew how much she loved being celebrated, wouldn't believe him, and would really come.

Panic rose in him. If their friends were outside their door tomorrow, Kate would be in New York the day after, and it would all begin again. If he didn't want that, he had to think of something. What lies did he need to keep their friends at bay?

He got out of the car, drank the last of the bottle, and threw it in a high arc into the forest. This was the way his life had always been: when he had to choose, it was always between two bad alternatives. Between life with his mother or his father when they finally separated. Between attending university, which cost him more money than he had and all his free time, or taking a job he hated, which would, however, give him time to write. Between Germany, where he had always felt a stranger, and America, where he remained just as much so. He wanted once and for all to have things be good, the way they were for other people. He wanted to be able to choose between good alternatives.

He didn't call their friends. He drove home, recounted his fruitless visit to the technician, said he wanted to try again tomorrow, if necessary with another technician in the next town over and with the phone company. Kate was irritated, not at him, but at life in the country, where the infrastructure couldn't hold a candle to New York. When she noticed this was upsetting him, she yielded. "Let's invest in our own infrastructure and put up a mast on the hill behind the house. We can afford it. Then we'll really be less dependent on technicians and phone companies."

8

He woke up in the middle of the night. It was a little before two a.m. He got up quietly and looked out the window through the curtains. The sky was clear and even without the moon, meadow, forest, and road were perfectly visible. In a single movement he picked up his clothes from the chair and tiptoed out of the room and down the creaking staircase. He got dressed in the kitchen, pulling a padded jacket over jeans and sweatshirt, a woolen cap over his head, and boots on his feet. It was cold outside; he'd seen the hoarfrost on the meadow.

The front door opened and closed quietly. He took the few steps to the car on tiptoe again. He put the key in the ignition and unlocked the steering wheel, then propped himself in the open door and pushed and steered the car from the meadow out onto the road. It was hard work, and he sighed and sweated. The car was soundless as it rolled across the grass. On the road the gravel crunched under the wheels and it seemed to him that the noise was deafening. But soon the road curved downward and the car began to move. He jumped in; after a few more curves he was out of earshot and turned on the engine.

On the trip to town, a few cars passed him in the opposite direction, but none, as far as he could see, that he recognized. In town, few windows were lit up, and he imagined a mother by the bed of a sick child or a father worrying about his business, or an old man who no longer needed his sleep.

All the windows were dark along the main street. He drove down it and didn't see a single person, no drunk on one of the benches, no lovers in one of the doorways. He drove past the sheriff's office; it was dark too, and there was a chain across the parking spaces for the two police cars. He switched off his headlights, drove slowly back, and stopped next to the blue sawhorses and police barricades. He waited to see if anything moved, then got out quietly and carefully lifted three sawhorses and two barricades into the flatbed. He got back in quietly, waited for a while again, then drove with his headlights off until he was clear of the town.

He turned on the radio. "We Are the Champions"—he had loved the song when he was a boy, and hadn't heard it for a long time. He sang along. Again he was filled with a sense of triumph. Once again he'd done it. There was more to him than other people realized. Than Kate realized. Than he himself believed most of the time. Once again he'd set things up so cleverly that nobody would be able to hang anything on him. An error, a prank—who was to know how the barrier had appeared on the road? Who wanted to know?

He drove, working out where to set up the roadblock. The road to his house branched off from the main road at a ninety-degree angle, made a sharp curve, and then ran almost parallel to the main road at first. It would be too noticeable to set up the barrier right where the road forked off, but it would work just as well along the curve.

It went quickly. He stopped after the curve, set up the saw-horses, and set up the barricades on the sawhorses. The road was blocked.

Before he'd reached the top of the rise that led to the house, he switched off the engine and the headlights. The car's momentum sufficed. Almost noiselessly and dark, the car rolled off the road and into the meadow. It was half past four.

He stayed sitting there and listened. He heard the wind in the trees and the occasional noise of an animal or a breaking twig. No sound came from the house. The first gray of dawn was not far off.

Kate asked, "Where were you?" But she wasn't fully awake. When she said to him the next morning that she'd thought he'd gone and then come back during the night, he shrugged his shoulders. "I was on the john."

9

In the days that followed he was happy. The happiness was tinged with anxiety. What if the sheriff found the barrier, what if a neighbor saw it and called it in, what if their friends refused to be blocked from reaching her? But no one came.

Once a day he removed one of the barricades, pushed a saw-horse aside, and drove the car through. He drove to the closed workshop again. He drove to the neighboring town and found a technician, whom, however, he didn't engage. He didn't call the phone company. Each time it felt good to remove the barricade and set it back again, push the sawhorse aside and then reposition it. Like being the lord of a castle, opening and closing the big gate.

He came back from his trips as fast as he could. Kate wanted to get to her desk, and he wanted to enjoy his world: the certain knowledge that Kate was upstairs writing, the joy of Rita being around him, the familiarity of their household routines. Because Thanksgiving was coming soon, he told Rita stories about the Pilgrim fathers and the Indians, and they painted a big picture in which everyone was celebrating together, the Pilgrims, the Indians, Kate, Rita, and himself.

"Are they coming to us? The fathers and the Indians?"

"No, Rita, they've been dead for a long time."

"But I want someone to come!"

"Me too." Kate was standing in the doorway. "I'm almost finished."

"With the book?"

She nodded. "With the book. And when I'm done, we'll celebrate. And invite our friends. And my agent and my editor. And the neighbors."

"Almost finished—what does that mean?"

"By the end of the week. Aren't you pleased?"

He went to her and took her in his arms. "Of course I'm pleased. It's a fantastic book. It will get wonderful reviews, it'll be in great piles at Barnes & Noble on the best-seller tables, and it'll make an amazing movie."

She lifted her head from his shoulder, leaned back, and

smiled at him. "You're so sweet. You've been so patient. You've taken care of me and Rita and the house and the garden, and it was the same thing day in, day out, and you never complained. Life's going to start up again now, I promise you."

He looked out the window at the kitchen garden, the wood-pile, and the compost heap. The edge of the pond was beginning to ice up; soon they'd be able to go skating. Wasn't that a life? What was she talking about?

"I'm going to drive into town on Monday—I have to go to the Internet café and also make some calls. Shall we have Thanksgiving here with our friends?"

"We can't invite them at such short notice. And how would Rita cope with so many grown-ups?"

"Everyone will love being allowed to read to Rita or play with her. She's every bit as sweet as you are."

What was she saying? He was as sweet as his daughter?

"I can also ask Peter and Liz if they want to bring their nephews. Probably her parents want to have them at Thanksgiving, but it can't hurt to ask. And my editor has a son who's the same age as Rita."

He was no longer listening to her. She'd betrayed him. She'd promised winter or spring, and instead she wanted to finish up now. In another few months her agent would have handed her the award at home over a glass of champagne, without any extravagance. Now the whole rumpus over the prize would let loose, merely a little late. Could he do anything to stop it? What would he have done until the end of winter or the beginning of spring? Could he have persuaded Kate to wait that long for the connection to be repaired and that he'd collect her e-mails from the Internet café in town? She trusted him with the mail, so why not with the e-mails too? Perhaps it would have begun to snow and never stopped, like in 1876, and they would have written and read and played and cooked and slept their way through the winter without any thought for the world outside.

"I'm going upstairs. The three of us will celebrate on Sunday, okay?"

10

Should he give up? But Kate had never been so much at peace, nor had she ever written so easily as in the last six months. She needed life here. So did Rita. He wasn't going to expose his little angel to the city traffic and the crime and the drugs. If he succeeded in giving Kate another child, or better, two, he would homeschool them. With just one child he thought it questionable, pedagogically speaking, but with two or three it was okay. And perhaps it was okay with one child too. Wasn't Rita being raised better by him and without any problems than she would be in some bad school?

On Sunday, Kate got up early; by late afternoon she was finished. "I've finished," she called, ran down the stairs, picked up Rita in one arm and took him in the other, and danced around the wooden pillars with them. Then she put on an apron. "Shall we cook? What have we got in the house? What would you like?"

Kate and Rita overflowed with boisterousness as they cooked and ate, laughing over the least little thing. "It'll end in tears," his grandmother had warned when her grandchildren's laughter became overexcited, and he wanted to warn Kate and Rita too. Then he felt he would be a sourpuss and let it be. But his mood got steadily darker. Their high spirits upset him.

"A story, a story," Rita begged after supper. Kate and he hadn't worked one out while they were cooking, but actually it was usually enough for one of them to start and then the other one took over while they listened to each other carefully. Today he hemmed and hawed until he'd spoiled Kate and Rita's pleasure in the story. While he felt bad about this, he wasn't able to rescue the mood again. And besides, it was time for Rita to go to bed.

"I'll take her," said Kate. He heard Rita laughing in the bathroom and jumping around in bed. When it quieted down, he waited for her to call him for her good-night kiss. But she didn't.

"She went straight to sleep," said Kate when she came to sit down with him. She didn't waste a word on his black mood. She was still elated, and the thought that she didn't even notice how he was feeling bad made him feel even worse. She was beaming, in a way she hadn't for a long time, her cheeks were glowing and her eyes shone. And she was holding herself and moving so self-confidently! She knows how beautiful she is and that she's too beautiful to be living in the country and belongs in New York, he thought, and his courage failed him.

"I'm driving to town after breakfast tomorrow—is there anything I can get you?"

"That's not going to work. I promised Jonathan to help repair the roof of the barn, and I need the car. You'd said you'd finish this weekend, and I thought you could stay with Rita tomorrow."

"But I said I want to go to town tomorrow."

"What I want doesn't count?"

"I didn't say that."

"That's what it sounded like."

"I'm sorry." She didn't want a fight, she wanted a solution. "I'll drop you off at Jonathan's and drive on to town."

"And Rita?"

"I'll take her with me."

"You know she gets sick in the car."

"Then I'll let her out with you—it's only twenty minutes to Jonathan's."

"Twenty minutes in the car for Rita are twenty minutes too many."

"Rita has got carsick twice, that's all. She had no problem in taxis in New York or in the car when we came here from New York. You have this fixed idea that she can't be in a car. Let's just try . . ."

"You want to do an experiment on Rita? Will she get sick or will she manage fine? No, Kate, you're not going to do an experiment on my daughter."

"Your daughter, your daughter . . . Rita is just as much my daughter as yours. Talk about Rita or about our daughter, but don't play the concerned father who has to protect his daughter against the bad mother."

"I'm not playing. I take care of Rita more than you do—that's all. If I say she's not going in the car, she's not going in the car."

"Why don't we ask her in the morning? She's pretty clear about what she wants."

"She's a little child, Kate. What if she wants to go in the car but can't cope with it?"

"Then I'll take her in my arms and carry her home."

He just shook his head. What she was saying was so idiotic that he felt he must actually go repair the barn roof with Jonathan. He stood up. "How about the half bottle of champagne that's in the fridge?" He kissed her on the head, brought the bottle and two glasses, and poured. "To you and your book!"

She produced a smile, raised her glass, and drank. "I think I'll go and take a last look at my book. Don't wait up for me."

11

He didn't wait up, and went to bed without her. But he lay awake until she was lying next to him. It was dark, he didn't say anything, breathed regularly, and after she'd been lying on her back for a while, as if wondering whether to wake him and talk to him, she turned on her side.

When he woke up the next morning, the bed was empty. He heard Kate and Rita in the kitchen, got dressed, and went downstairs.

"Papa, I'm allowed to go in the car!"

"No, Rita, it makes you ill. We'll wait for that till you're bigger and stronger."

"But Mummy said . . ."

"Mummy meant later, not now."

"Don't tell me what I mean." Kate's voice was controlled. But then suddenly her control was used up and she screamed at him. "The shit you talk! You say you want to help Jonathan with the barn, and you sleep in half the morning? You say you want to go skiing with Rita in the winter and you think riding in the car is too dangerous? You want to turn me into Mummy at her stove, waiting for Daddy to be gracious enough to let her have the car? Either the three of us drive to Jonathan's now and I let you out there, or Rita and I go alone."

"I want to turn you into Mummy at her stove? What am I, if not Daddy at the stove? Just a failed writer? Who lives on your money? Who takes care of your daughter but isn't allowed to decide anything? Nanny and cleaning lady?"

Kate had got herself under control again. She looked at him with raised eyebrows. "You know I don't mean any of that. I'm leaving now—are you coming?"

"You're not leaving!"

But she put on her jacket and shoes, and Rita's, and went to the door. When he blocked the two of them from going out the front door, Kate picked up Rita and went out through the veranda. He hesitated, ran after Kate, caught up to her, and grabbed her. Then Rita started to cry and he let go. He followed Kate off the veranda and across the meadow to the car.

"Please don't do this!"

Kate didn't answer, got into the driver's seat with Rita on the passenger seat beside her, pulled the door shut, and switched on the engine.

"But not in the front seat!" He wanted to open the door, but Kate pressed the lock. He banged against the door, seized the handle, and tried to stop the car. It drove off. He ran alongside, and saw that Rita was kneeling up on the front seat, staring at him terrified with a tearstained face. "The seat belt," he called, "put on Rita's seat belt!" But Kate didn't react, the car gathered speed, and he had to let go.

He ran behind the car but couldn't catch up with it. Kate wasn't driving fast on the dirt road but was still leaving him behind, and with every yard of road between two curves the distance lengthened. Then the car was gone, and he heard it further and further away.

He ran on. He had to chase after the car, even if he could no longer catch up with it. He had to run to remain in his life, in his wife's, and in his daughter's. He had to run, so as not to have to return to the empty house. He had to run, so as not to stand still.

Finally, he couldn't go on. He bent forward, with his hands on his knees. When he was finally calmer and could hear something aside from his own breathing, he heard the sound of the car in the far distance. He straightened up, but couldn't see it. The noise hung there, slowly faded, and he waited for it to

cease altogether. Instead he heard a far-off crash. Then everything was still.

He started running again. He imagined the car, which had
hit the barricades and the sawhorses or a tree because Kate
had wrenched the steering wheel to the side, he saw Kate's and
Rita's bloodied heads against the shattered windshield, Kate
tumbling onto the road with Rita in her arms, cars driving past
heedlessly, he heard Rita screaming and Kate sobbing. Or were
the two of them trapped, unable to get out, and any moment
the gas would ignite and the car explode? He ran on, although
his legs could barely carry him, and there were daggers in his
chest and side.

Then he saw the car. Thank God it wasn't on fire. It was
empty, and Kate and Rita were nowhere to be seen, neither
near the car nor on the main road. He waited, waved, but wasn't
picked up. He went back to the car, saw that it had hit the barricades and sawhorse, and that the sawhorse was wedged so
tightly between the bumper and the underside of the car that
it couldn't move anymore. The door was open, and he got into
the driver's seat. The windshield wasn't shattered, but in one
spot there was a smear of blood, not in front of the driver but
on the passenger's side.

The ignition worked when he turned the key, but when he
put the car into reverse, it dragged the trapped sawhorse with
it. He tied the sawhorse firmly to a tree with the rope, backed
up, then rolled forward, backward, then forward, again and
again. It struck him that this was his punishment for destroy-
ing the phone lines, and when the car finally freed itself from
the sawhorse he was utterly exhausted, just like before. He
loaded the barricades and sawhorses into the cargo area and
drove to the hospital. Yes, his wife and daughter had been
brought in half an hour ago. He had them tell him where
to go.

12

The hallways were more pleasant than those he remembered in German hospitals, broad, with leather chairs and flower arrangements. A poster in the elevator announced that the hospital had been made Hospital of the Year again for the fourth time in a row. He was asked to go into a waiting room, the doctor would be with him shortly, he sat down, stood up again, looked at the colorful photographs on the walls, found the ruins of Cambodian and Mexican temples depressing, sat down again. After half an hour the door opened and the doctor introduced himself. He was young, energetic, and cheerful.

"There's luck in bad luck. Your wife held her right arm in front of your daughter," he put his right arm out, "and when your daughter was thrown against it with full force, it broke. But it's a clean break, and it may have saved your daughter's life. In addition your wife has three broken ribs and a whiplash injury. But they'll heal. We'll just keep her here for a few days." He laughed. "It's an honor to have the American Book Prize winner as a patient, and it was such a pleasure to be the bearer of good news. I recognized her immediately, I hardly dared speak to her—and she knew nothing about it and was thrilled."

"How is my daughter?"

"She has a laceration on her forehead that we stitched up, and she's resting. We'll observe her tonight, and if there are no problems, you can take her home tomorrow."

He nodded. "Can I see my wife?"

"I'll take you there."

She was in a single room, her neck and right arm encased in some white synthetic material. The doctor left the two of them alone.

He pulled a chair up to the bed. "Congratulations on the prize."

"You knew. You were in town almost every day, and when you're in town, you read the *New York Times*. Why didn't you tell me? Because you're not a successful writer, I'm not allowed to be one either?"

"No, Kate, I just wanted to keep our world here in one piece. I'm not jealous. You can write as many best sellers . . ."

"I don't think I'm better than you. You deserve the same success, and I'm sorry the world is unjust and doesn't give you that same success. But I can't stop writing just because of that. I can't diminish myself."

"Down to my size?" He shook his head. "I didn't want the whole circus to start up again, the interviews and talk shows and parties and all the rest of it. To have it all become the way it was before. Our six months here have been so good for us."

"I can't stand it if all that's left of me is a shadow that disappears to its desk every morning and sits by the fire with you every evening and plays families once a week."

"We don't sit by the fire, we talk, and we're not playing families, we are one."

"You know what I mean—what I've been for you these past six months is what any woman could have been who's preoccupied and doesn't say much and likes to snuggle up at night. I can't live with a man whose jealousy won't allow me to be anything more than that. Or doesn't love anything about me but that."

"What's that supposed to mean?"

"We're leaving you. We're moving . . ."

"You? You and Rita? Rita, whom I've washed and dressed and cooked for and taught to read and write? Whom I've taken care of when she was ill? No judge will give you custody."

"After that attack of yours today?"

"My attack . . ." He shook his head again. "That wasn't an attack. I only tried to block things off, the phone and the Internet and even the road."

"It was an attack, and the driver who brought me here is going to notify the sheriff."

He had been sitting on the chair with his back hunched and his head low. Now he straightened up. "I sorted out the car, I drove it here, and the roadblock has gone. All the sheriff is going to find out is that you drove our daughter without a car seat or a seat belt." He looked at his wife. "No judge will give you Rita. You have to stay with me."

What was in her eyes as she looked back at him? Hatred? Not possible. A refusal to understand. It wasn't her broken arm and broken ribs that were hurting her. What was hurting her was that he'd torpedoed her plan. She didn't want to recognize that she couldn't make plans without him. It was time she finally learned. He stood up. "I love you, Kate."

What right did she have to look at him in horror? What right did she have to say: "You've gone mad."

13

He drove through town along the main street. He would have liked to put the barricades and sawhorses unobtrusively back on the pile, but the town fair was over and the piles had been cleared away.

He called the phone company from the general store and reported the damaged lines. They promised to send a repair crew the same afternoon.

In the house he went from room to room. In the bedroom

he opened the curtains and the window, made the bed, and folded the nightshirt and pajamas. In Kate's study he remained standing in the doorway. She had tidied up; the desk was clear except for the computer and the printer and a printed stack of paper, and the books and papers that had been lying on the floor were back on the shelves. It looked as if she'd closed not just the book but a part of her life, and it made him sad. Rita's room smelled of little girl; he shut his eyes, sniffed, and smelled her bear, which he wasn't allowed to wash, her shampoo, her sweat. In the kitchen he loaded dishes and pots into the dishwasher and left everything else where it was: the sweater, as if Kate could walk in at any moment and pull it on, the paints, as if Rita were about to sit down at the table and keep painting. He felt cold, and turned up the heat.

He stepped outside. No judge was going to take Rita away from him. In the worst case, the right lady lawyer would get him generous alimony. And then he would live here in the mountains on his own with Rita. And Rita would grow up with a mother who lived a five-hour drive away. Kate wants to push things to the limit? Let her find out what she gets out of that.

He looked out at the forest, the meadow with the apple trees and lilacs, and the pond with the weeping willows. No skating all together on the frozen pond? No sledding all together on the slope beyond the far bank? Even if Rita managed emotionally without her mother, and he managed financially—he didn't want to lose this world that sometimes had felt in summer as though it had always been his and always would be.

He would work out a plan for keeping his world together. It would be a joke if he couldn't, given the good cards in his hand. Tomorrow he could collect Rita. In a few days Rita and he would be in front of the hospital waiting for Kate. With flowers. And a sign saying "Welcome home." And their love.

He went to the car, unloaded the barricades and sawhorses, and carried them to the spot behind the kitchen where he chopped and sawed up the wood for the fire. He worked until darkness, pulling the nails out of the sawhorses and chopping and sawing the barricades and braces into pieces. In the light that fell there from the kitchen window he stacked the wood into the pile, removing some of the logs he'd already stored for the winter and packing the new pieces between them.

He filled the basket with new and old wood and carried it inside to the fireplace. The phone rang; the phone company was calling to let him know the line was working again. He checked with the hospital and was told that Kate and Rita were asleep and there was nothing to worry about.

Then the fire was burning. He sat in front of it and watched as the pieces of wood caught alight, burned, glowed, and fell apart. On one of the blue ones he could read "Line" in white letters, part of the inscription "Police Line Do Not Cross." The fire melted the paint, wiping out the inscription and consuming it. This is how he wanted to be sitting in front of the fire with Kate and Rita in a few weeks. Kate would read "Not" or "Do" on one of the pieces of wood and remember today. She would understand how much he loved her and slide over to him and cuddle up.

Stranger in the Night

1

"You recognized me, didn't you?" No sooner had he sat down next to me than he started talking. He was the last passenger; the stewardesses closed the doors behind him.

"We . . ." We had stood with other passengers at the bar in the lounge. Rain beat against the windows, the New York–Frankfurt flight had been postponed several times, and we passed the time overcoming our irritation with champagne and tales of delayed flights and missed opportunities.

He didn't give me time to reply. "I saw it in your eyes. I know that look: first it's a question, then it's recognition, then it's disgust. Where did you—Stupid question, at the end my story was in all the papers and on every TV channel."

I looked over at him. He was roughly fifty, tall and lean, with a pleasant, intelligent face, and black hair going rapidly gray. He hadn't told any stories at the bar; the only thing I'd noticed was his loose-hanging, softly creased suit.

"I'm sorry"—why was I saying I was sorry?—"I don't recognize you." The plane took off and climbed steeply. I like the minutes when your back is pressed against your seat and you feel it in your stomach and your body senses that it's flying. Through the window I looked down at the city's sea of lights. Then the plane banked in a wide curve, all I saw was sky, until eventually the sea was below me with the moonlight glowing off it.

My neighbor laughed softly. "People keep recognizing me and I keep denying it. And now I wanted to take the bull by the horns, but there's no bull." He laughed again and introduced himself. "Werner Menzel. I hope we have a good flight!"

Over drinks we exchanged empty pleasantries, over dinner we watched different movies. Nothing prepared me for him to turn to me as the cabin lights were dimmed: "Are you very tired? I know I have no right to burden you, but if I may tell you my story—it won't take long." He stopped, laughed again softly. "No, it will actually take long, but I'd really appreciate it. You know, up to now it's been the media telling my story. But that wasn't my story, it was theirs. My story doesn't exist yet. I have to learn how to tell it. What better way could there be than to tell it to someone who hasn't heard any part of it, a stranger in the night."

I'm not one of those people who find it impossible to sleep in planes. But I didn't want to be unfriendly. Besides which there was something in the way he said "stranger in the night," some ironic tenderness, that moved and seduced me.

2

"The story starts back before the Iraq War. I had a job in the Ministry of Trade and was invited to join a circle of young colleagues from the Ministry of the Interior, the Foreign Ministry, and the university. A reading and discussion group—the salon was back in fashion in Berlin at the time. We met every four weeks at eight in the evening, had discussions, emptied several bottles of wine, and at eleven we were often joined by our girlfriends on their way back from work, a concert, or the theater, to make fun of our bookishness and enjoy the last moments of our conversations. It was often the most lively right at the end.

"Sometimes our diplomats invited us to their receptions, not the important ones, but the one with foreign poets or artists. To begin with my girlfriend and I stuck with the people we already knew. Then we realized that other people were glad if we started talking to them. Naturally there were some who were too important for us to be interesting to them, and others who just behaved that way. But they were exceptions. I would never have thought it—you can really have fun at a reception.

"I should have noticed—I noticed that the attaché from the Kuwaiti Embassy was flirting with my girlfriend. Should I have taken that as a reason to avoid contact? He was a playful flirt, he was more admiring of her beauty than seriously courting her. That's the way I flirt too if a woman attracts me—letting her know she's attractive rather than trying to get her. My girlfriend flirted back; she was not really encouraging him, just showing that she enjoyed his compliments."

While he was talking he had propped his elbow on the armrest, but now he leaned back.

"She was incredibly beautiful. I was in love with her blond hair! Its pale and dark streaks, the way it fell onto her shoulders in waves, the way it lit her face with its own glow. 'My angel,' I kept wanting to say, 'my angel.' And her figure!" I heard him laugh again softly. "You know how self-hating women can be about their own bodies. Perhaps her calves were a little plump, but I liked them. They anchored her blond beauty. They went with the fact that her grandfather was a farmer and her father was a railroad guy and she was a very hands-on doctor. I also liked it that by a quirk of nature the space between her nose and her upper lip was a little short, which often made her mouth open just a fraction. It gave her this bewitchingly charming expression, like a child dazzled by the world. But when she was concentrating and her lips were closed, her face showed the strength of her determination. Oh, and the way she walked—do you know the song 'Elle ne marche pas, elle danse'?" He hummed the melody quietly.

"We shouldn't have accepted the attaché's invitation. But my girlfriend loved foreign travel, and I, who don't like traveling . . . Crazy, isn't it? I don't like to travel, would have preferred not to travel back then, and because I did travel, now I have to travel to save my life. So I thought I owed it to her to make the trip, and was pleased that at least we weren't going to be stupid tourists, but would have a local partner and a place to stay. No one had given us any warnings, and why should they? We accepted the invitation and flew at Easter.

"We stayed in a hotel, not in the grounds where the attaché and his clan had their houses and courtyards and gardens. I thought it was already enough that he was looking after us. We were always going somewhere with him, and often his brothers and his friends. We drove into the desert, to the oil fields, and went out to sea with fishermen, we visited the university and the parliament and gambled and won at the camel races. It wasn't an adventure, it was a rich people's holiday; the infrastructure is like Florida's, the restaurants have French cooks, picnics are served at picnic tables with tablecloths, porcelain, and silver, and we were driven around in large chauffeured cars. It was impressive. But I was glad when we were back in the evenings in our suite. Or when we sat out on the balcony in the mornings and watched the sunrise. Whether on the Mediterranean or the North Sea, we had often watched the sun sink into the water, but we had never seen it come rising out of it."

3

He put his hand on my arm. "You're very patient. Shall we have a glass of red wine? You had the Bordeaux, but the Russian River Valley Pinot Noir is better." He didn't wait for my answer but pressed the call button and persuaded the stewardess to leave us with the whole bottle. He sounded cheerful, as if the memories and the story had animated him.

"One morning they couldn't collect us, and we wanted to take a taxi. At the entrance to the driveway we were hailed by two men who had been having breakfast at the next table and with whom we had exchanged newspapers. Could they give us a lift into the city? We got in, my girlfriend in front, me behind, and set off; at a red light the driver asked me please to jump out and drop a letter in the mailbox. Why me, you will ask, why didn't he ask the other man or get out himself? The other man limped, as I'd immediately noticed, and the driver was on the left and the mailbox on the right; I could almost have reached out the window and dropped the letter in. So I got out, and the light turned green, and the car drove off. There was a lot of traffic; I thought, the driver doesn't want to hold things up, he'll drive around the block and come right back."

He stopped, and switched off the little lights in the ceiling that shone down on his seat and mine. Did he want me not to see his pain? I said nothing, gripped his hand, and squeezed it briefly.

"Yes, he didn't come back. I stood there and after half an hour I called the attaché. He phoned the minister and the minister immediately called out the police and blocked off the roads and increased security at the airport and alerted the coast guard. I was taken to police headquarters and shown hundreds of photographs. I didn't recognize either of the men. The German ambassador and his wife picked me up and took me to their official residence; they didn't want me to be alone in the circumstances. Everyone was alert and friendly and protective.

"The first night I didn't sleep. But a new day brings new courage, and I was full of hope as I got out of bed. I got out of bed full of hope on the next days, too. Until I had to admit to myself how bad things looked. The ambassador told me what he knew about the white slave trade in the Near East. When I was back in Germany I read everything on it I could find. In earlier times there were trading centers or markets, if you will, where the abducted women were sold and where you could try to buy yours back at auction. Today the women are secretly videoed, interested parties look at these on the Internet and make offers and order the women online, and only then are the women abducted. If her husband or boyfriend or the police notice, all traces are erased.

"What happens to the women, you'll ask. We're talking about top-grade women and top prices. If the women go along, they're treated well. If they don't go along, they change hands several times and end up in a whorehouse in Mombasa."

I tried to put myself in his place. How does one mourn a beloved woman for whom one can only hope that she feels fine in someone else's arms? Whom one can get back only when even a drunken sailor in Mombasa no longer wants her? How long does one mourn? How long does one wait?

4

"A year later the Iraq War started. I didn't think it had anything to do with me or vice versa. But in Kuwait the rich families panicked and moved out, to Los Angeles or Cannes or Geneva or wherever they had houses.

"She got away from him in Geneva. She climbed out a window, clambered over a fence, stopped a car on the street, and called me immediately, using the driver's phone. I caught the next plane. Because she was afraid they could search for her and find her, she didn't want to be alone, and the driver, a student, took her to the reading room at the university library. She sat there till I came.

"Do you know the University Library in Geneva? A magnificent building with a reading room that looks like something out of a turn-of-the-century picture book. She was sitting in the middle of the first row, conspicuously dressed, made up, perfumed. As I arrived at her table, she held her head down. I touched her arm and she looked up and screamed. Then she recognized me."

The pilot announced from the cockpit that there was turbulence ahead and told us to fasten our seat belts and pull them tight. The stewardesses went down the rows, checking to see that the pilot's instructions were being followed, waking sleeping passengers whose blankets were covering their seat belts and collecting glasses.

My seatmate stopped talking and watched what was going on. "They're serious. I've never seen the stewardesses wake passengers in first class." He looked at me. "Do you feel afraid when things get dangerous on a flight? Or do you believe in

God? Who will not let you fall without catching you? I don't believe in God. I don't believe in God and I don't know if I still believe in justice and truth. I used to think that people who don't have long to live tell the truth. But perhaps people who don't have long to live are the worst liars. If they don't play to the gallery now, then when? Truth . . . what is truth without a judge to sign and seal it? And what is a lie when he does? What is truth if it's just wandering through people's heads and authoritative corroboration?" Again he laughed his quick, soft laugh. "Forgive me, I'm a bit addled. I get afraid when flying turns dangerous, and what's happening right now spells danger. But I must stop talking like Pontius Pilate or Raskolnikov, otherwise you'll be asking yourself why you have to listen to me."

Then it was as if a large hand seized the plane to play with it. It shook it, dropped it, caught it again, then dropped it again. The seat belt held my body but my insides felt as if they'd lost their place; I put my hands on my stomach to hold them tight. On the other side of the aisle a woman vomited, in front of me a man called for help, and behind me pieces of luggage came crashing down. Only when the plane resumed its peaceful flight did fear strike, not just fear of what had happened but fear of what might still be to come. It wasn't over yet. The plane dropped again and gravity exerted its pull again on the body and its organs.

5

"That's just how it was when we were together again. We were shaken and torn. It was like a poison. Sometimes everything went along calmly, but we didn't trust each other. We eyed each other suspiciously till one of us couldn't take it anymore, then things would get cold and cutting and loud and rough."

He was talking again? What was he talking about?

"You were shaken and torn. By what?"

"That's how it felt. Like the storm that's shaking our plane. A force that's more powerful than we are. We fell into each other's arms in the reading room and I held her in my arms all night that first night and the nights that followed, and we moved in together, which we hadn't trusted ourselves sufficiently to do before, and we thought everything would be fine. But she didn't want to make love with me, and at first I thought, she's traumatized, like after a rape, and needs time and tenderness and being cared for, but then I asked myself, does she still love me? Had a piece of her heart stayed with the attaché? Had things finally been not so bad with him?"

"With the attaché?"

"Yes, he was the one who had her abducted."

"The attaché? Has he been sentenced?"

"She needed a temporary identity card to be able to fly from Geneva to Berlin, and we drove to the German ambassador in Bern and told him the whole thing. He spoke to the Swiss police, who said we should talk to the German police in Germany. The German police said they could only turn to the Swiss police. Nobody wanted political trouble with Kuwait. We could have gone to the media; after an article in *Bild* and an interview in *Stern* maybe the police and the Foreign Office would have done something. But we didn't want to hand ourselves over to the media."

"You suspected your girlfriend although she . . ."

"Although she ran away?" He nodded several times. "I understand your question. I've kept asking myself the same thing. But being overpowered and abducted and used can have its own sexual attraction, for women as for men. She had flirted with him and he with her. She didn't want to spend her life in his harem so she had to escape. But that doesn't mean she didn't have the sexual experience of her life with him. And her refusing to sleep with me and my suspecting her wasn't the whole thing, either. She suspected me too. I had put her in danger by going to Kuwait, and I hadn't done all I could have done after she was abducted."

The cabin lights came on, and the stewardesses took care of the vomit on the other side of the aisle, the whimpering passenger in front of me, and the fallen luggage behind. My seatmate kept talking, but I was concentrating on the rumble of the engines, which didn't sound right, and was no longer listening to him. Till I heard him say:

"But she was dead."

"Dead?"

"It was only two floors up, and I thought she'd broken something, her legs or an arm. But she was dead. She landed on her head."

"How—"

"I pushed her, but she'd hit me. I was only trying to fend her off, I didn't want to get hit again. I know I shouldn't have pushed her. We shouldn't have been fighting. But we fought a lot then, it's pretty much all we did anymore. Nor was it the first time we'd gone for each other physically. But it was the first time on the balcony, and my girlfriend was tall and the railing was low. I grabbed for her arms and tried to hold her, but she smacked my hands away." He shook his head. "I think she didn't realize the danger and didn't know what she was doing. But I don't know. What if she preferred to die than to let me save her?"

6

I grabbed his hand again and squeezed it. How could anyone live with a question like that? But then it wasn't just the rumble of the engines that sounded wrong. "Didn't you say your story was in all the newspapers and on all the TV channels? The media aren't interested in a fall from a balcony!"

He took his time. "There was also the matter of the money."

"Money?"

"Well," he spoke slowly and awkwardly. "The attaché had told her he'd bought her from me. She didn't really believe it, but it still preoccupied her, and she sometimes asked me about it and sometimes also talked to her girlfriend. After she died the girlfriend told the police."

"That was all?"

"The police found the money in my account. As soon as the three million was deposited, I tried to send it back. But it had been paid in cash in Singapore or Delhi or Dubai, and couldn't be returned."

"Someone simply deposited three million in your account?"

He sighed. "When we got to know each other, the attaché sometimes made jokes and played the Bedouin who still lives according to his ancient customs. Ah, beautiful blond woman! Swap woman? Want camels? I played along and we bargained and haggled. We set the price of a camel at three thousand, and I drove the price of my girlfriend up to a thousand camels. It was a game."

I didn't believe my ears. "A game? In which you finally laughed and said okay and struck a deal? And when you went to Kuwait, you didn't worry that the game could turn serious?"

"Worry? No, I wasn't worried. I was a bit curious to see if he'd take the game further and show me a thousand camels or offer me racehorses or sports cars. I was tickled, but I wasn't worried." He put his hand on my arm again. "I know I made a dreadful mistake. But if you knew the attaché, you'd understand me. Educated at an English public school, cultivated, witty, cosmopolitan—I genuinely thought we were playing a harmless intercultural game."

"But when your girlfriend disappeared—in any case when the money arrived, you knew who had her. When did it arrive?"

"When I came back from Kuwait, it was in my account. What should I have done? Fly back to Kuwait and tell the attaché to take his money back and give me back my girlfriend? And when he laughed in my face, complain to the emir? Beg our foreign minister to talk to the emir? Hire a couple of guys from the Russian mafia and invade the estate where the attaché lived and was probably holding her captive? I know, a real man who loves his wife busts her out. And if he dies doing it, he dies. Better to die with dignity than live as a coward. I also know that with three million I had enough money to organize the Russians and the weapons and the helicopter and whatever else you need. But that's out of the movies. That's not my world. I'm not up to it. The guys from the Russian mafia would simply take my money, and the weapons would all be rusty, and the helicopter would have gearbox trouble."

7

I had forgotten the engine. But the pilot had also heard the wrong rumbling and perhaps he'd also seen little lights come on and indicators go wild. He announced from the cockpit that we would be landing in Reykjavik in an hour. There was no cause for alarm, it was only a small problem, we could fly to Frankfurt with it, but to be on the safe side, he wanted to have it checked out in Reykjavik.

The announcement made some passengers uneasy. No cause for alarm? Why would he be landing if we were okay to keep flying? Maybe in fact we couldn't keep flying? In which case, wasn't the situation in fact dangerous? Others started telling one another what they knew about Reykjavik and Iceland, the summers when it never got dark, the winters when it never got light, the geysers and the sheep, the island ponies and the island moss. Seat backs were raised, tables and monitors opened, stewardesses summoned. The passengers became cheerful, noisy, busy, until one of them noticed black smoke coming out of one of the engines. The news went from mouth to mouth, and each person who passed it on then stopped talking. Soon there was silence on the plane.

My seatmate whispered, "Maybe in the storm a bolt of lightning hit an engine? I've heard it's quite common."

"Yes." I was whispering too. It seemed to me that I could hear the engine grinding, as if something had inserted itself into the turbines and it was trying in vain to grind it into little pieces. As if it were wounded and exhausted and couldn't keep going. I was afraid, and the sound of the wounded machinery was like the groaning of a wounded man. "What did you do with the money?"

"I know I shouldn't have touched it, I should have left it there. But I have a knack with money. I've always invested what little money I had, and beat every benchmark and every index." He raised his arms in apology. "Now I had real money. Now I could finally get going. In three years I turned the three million into five. What use would it have been to anyone if the money

hadn't been put to work? To no one. Do you know the parable
of the talents? About the man who gives each of his servants
ten pounds and after he comes back he rewards the two servants who've put the money to work and punishes the servant
who's just let it lie? For unto every one that hath shall be given,
and he shall have abundance: but from him that hath not shall
be taken away even that which he hath. That's the way it is.

"But in court I realized that other people don't understand
it at all." He shook his head. "The judges talked to me as if
I'd really sold my girlfriend. Why else would I have taken the
money and worked with it? As if I'd killed her. Had she worked
it all out and threatened me or blackmailed me? The prosecutor couldn't prove a thing. Until the neighbor surfaced."

8

I couldn't watch the engine and the black smoke, but I was listening to the grinding noise. Till it stopped. At that moment a
sigh ran through the plane, a collective sigh as the passengers
saw a burst of flame shoot out.

My seatmate trembled and held tight to the armrests with
both hands. "I can't help myself, flying frightens me, even after
I've flown around the globe I don't know how many times. We
weren't created to fly through the heavens and fall to earth or
into the sea from thirty thousand feet. Yet my head gives its
total assent to death in a plane crash. You know it's about to
happen, you have a last glass of champagne, you say goodbye to
life, and boom—it's over." He had been whispering again, but
when he said "boom" his voice rose and he clapped his hands.
The stewardess came and he ordered champagne. "You too?"

I shook my head.

After the stewardess had poured him a glass, he started talking again. "You know, I begin to feel at home in a new house or a new neighborhood only when I get to know people. When I know all about the life of the woman in the newspaper shop and I don't have to tell her what I want each morning. When I know the pharmacist so well that he gives me my prescription medicine without a prescription. When the Italian restaurant a few houses down the road makes me a pasta that's not on the menu.

"The neighbor who can see my balcony from hers is an old lady who has trouble walking and even more trouble carrying things; I often helped her across the street and up the stairs with her shopping. I like her, and she likes me too. During the trial she calls me up and invites me over and says she hopes she's mistaken but can only say in court what she saw, and to her at least it looked like not only did I push my girlfriend but I forced her over the balcony. The neighbor had fought with herself about what to do and told me she was sorry and she was sure everything would clear itself up. Was it really me who'd been fighting with my girlfriend on the evening in question? She hadn't been able to recognize me.

"What chance would my defense attorney have had with the court against an adorable old lady, a retired teacher, alert and lucid, and who also liked me? On top of it all an old friend of my girlfriend's, a journalist, got into the act and ensured that the case made headlines and I looked bad. You know the kind of old friends women sometimes have? From school or even from kindergarten? Who don't end up with the woman but cling to her obsequiously all through life? And make the woman wonder why her actual partner isn't as clinging and obsequious as they are? He didn't like me even without knowing a single thing about the whole thing. It was enough that my girlfriend and I were together.

"I didn't want to go to prison. Because I was only accused of negligent homicide I wasn't taken into custody and my money wasn't seized. I got the money transferred to the Virgin Islands and myself out of Germany the night before the old lady was due to testify."

I couldn't let it alone. "Did you love your girlfriend? She doesn't even have a name in your story."

"Ava. Her mother was mad about Ava Gardner. Yes, I loved her. She was gorgeous and we never had any problems. I mean till we had the real problem. Going places with her, to a reception or a premiere or even just a restaurant or driving through town in a convertible or out into the country or wandering around the market or having a vacation in a hotel on the beach—we were a very visible couple and we liked being noticed. Does that sound a little superficial? Less like passion and more like vanity? It wasn't superficial. We both loved the good life. We both liked it when the world was beautiful and we were a beautiful part of it. We didn't just like it, we loved it passionately. It was a different sort of passion, not Romeo and Juliet, not Sturm und Drang. But it was a genuine, deep passion."

"But when it wasn't all beautiful anymore, why didn't you leave? Why didn't you let Ava leave?"

"I don't understand it either. When she began to cross-examine me and accuse me of things and judge me, I just wouldn't stand for it. I had to defend myself, I had to attack her back. I wanted her to respect me."

"Did you apologize to her?"

"She wanted me to."

I waited, but he didn't answer my question. Before I could decide whether to ask again or let it be, the plane gave a gentle shudder and touched down on the runway in Reykjavik.

9

The stewardess said welcome to Reykjavik, the local time is two a.m. The runways were empty, the buildings dark, and the plane soon reached the gate. We were told to take our hand luggage with us as another plane might be sent to pick us up.

Even in this situation correct form was observed; we first-class passengers were led from the upper deck to the lower deck and out of the plane while the passengers from the other two sections waited. In the lounge, which had been opened up specially, the first-class and business-class passengers sat together. The same first-class passengers who'd been standing at the bar in New York were now standing at the bar here. There was no champagne, and anyone who didn't have his own story of a plane crash or a plane near-crash to tell listened dully to someone else's. Why should they be interested in dangers that other people had escaped?

Once again my seatmate was standing there wordlessly. I sometimes looked over at him and he smiled back, and his smile was as faint and soft as his laugh. Otherwise I listened to the stories. Till a glass broke on the floor. The narrator interrupted his tale and his listeners turned their heads. My seatmate was the one whose glass had fallen, but he didn't bend over to pick up the shards, nor did he wipe the stains from his pants. He didn't move.

I went to him and put my hand on his back. "Can I help you?"

He had trouble seeing me and responding. "He . . . he is . . ." He felt everyone looking at him and stopped. A waiter came and swept up the fragments and wiped up the wine. I tried to lead my seatmate to the window, where it was quieter, but he declined with an oddly querulous tone in his voice. "No, not the window." I looked around. It was also quieter over by the newspaper rack.

"Should I ask them to put out a call for a doctor?"

"A doctor . . . no, a doctor can't help." He took a couple of deep breaths in and out, then he got hold of himself again. "Over there by the window, the man in the pale suit—I knew he was following me, but I thought I was one or two flights ahead of him. A couple of years ago he took a shot at me. I don't know if he wanted to shoot me and I just got lucky, or whether he wanted to put me on notice."

"He took a shot at you? Did you press charges?"

"Hospitals call the police when they have cases of gunshot wounds. I described him and looked at photos again but it went nowhere. In Cape Town, where it happened, there's a lot of shooting, and the police thought maybe I just got caught in the crossfire. I knew better. But what good would it have done to tell that to the police?"

I waited to see if he'd explain.

"When I left Germany, I flew from one place to another and eventually stopped in Cape Town. If you have money and behave yourself properly, in South Africa they leave you alone. I rented the gatehouse of a winery on the edge of Cape Town, with the sea on one side and the vineyards on the other, a miniature paradise. But after a few months his letter arrived. He hadn't written his name as sender on the back of the envelope, he didn't have to. The story he sent me said it all. A woman runs away from the sheikh with another man. She's his darling, the apple of his eye, as young and beautiful as the dawn. The sheikh is sad, but although he's a proud man he has a big heart, and understands that a woman who loves must follow her heart. Years later the man kills the woman in anger. The sheikh, who has tolerated his property going its own way, will not tolerate that property's destruction by someone else. So he has the other man killed.

"Next morning when I turned my car out of the estate onto the road, the man in the pale suit was standing on the other side. He always wears a pale suit, and the suit is always a little too big for him. He could look pathetic and ridiculous, but there's a threat implicit in the way he holds himself and moves and the way he walks, and he doesn't look pathetic and ridiculous, he looks dangerous. In the rearview mirror I saw him cross the road and get into a car, and shortly afterward I saw the car tailing mine."

10

He took a few steps to a chair, turned it so that he couldn't see the man in the pale suit, sat down with his arms on his knees, folded his hands, and hung his head. I fetched another chair and sat down facing him.

"Then he shot at you in Cape Town?"

"In the next weeks I saw him repeatedly. He was leaning on the lamppost opposite the restaurant where I ate, he was standing outside the bookstore I was coming out of and outside which he hadn't been standing when I went in, he was sitting opposite me when I looked up from the newspaper on the bus. I had the sea right outside my door, and every morning and every evening I took a long walk along the shore. One evening he was coming toward me, and after that I stayed in the house. But I did have to go out sometimes, and while I was shopping for groceries in Cape Town, he shot at me. In full daylight in the middle of the street.

"After a few days in the hospital I started taking planes again and zigzagged until I finally hoped I had shaken him off. And it took him a whole year to find me again."

I looked over at the man in the pale suit. He fixed his eyes on me as if we were playing that child's game when you have to look at each other and hold your gaze without blinking. After a while I looked away.

My seatmate smiled. "What a year! I love the sea and I found another house on the beach, this time in California. In America, too, if you have money and behave properly, you can live unrecognized and nobody bothers you. At first it was irritating not to be able to use my credit cards; they leave a trace. But if you're not in a hurry you can manage without them. The man renting out the property preferred cash to plastic anyway; probably he was cheating on his taxes.

"Do you know the coast north of San Francisco? Sometimes cliff-strewn and raw, then sandy and gentle again, the Pacific colder and more pitiless than any other ocean, the mountains plunging down to the water all shrouded in mist in the mornings, then their dry brown grass turning them to molten gold in the afternoon and evening sun—it's as if the world in all its beauty were created every day anew. My house was on the slope, so far below the road that I didn't hear the traffic and so close to the sea that the sound of the waves accompanied me from morning to nightfall, not loudly and threateningly, but quietly, in a conciliatory way. And oh! The sunsets! I was particularly captivated by them when they flared in reds and pinks; they were paintings of sumptuous beauty. But I was also moved by others in their restraint, when the sun submerges itself in the haze over the water and disappears without a trace."

He laughed quietly, a little ironic, a little embarrassed. "Have I become someone who goes into raptures? Yes, I have! I could go on being rapturous: about the rich, salty air and the storms and the rainbows over the ocean and the wine. And about Debbie, who was blond and beautiful and didn't just go through life, she danced. She was Ava's reincarnation, but while Ava in the end wished me harm, Debbie wished me well. She lived half an hour further along the road, had a house on the mountain, a horse and a dog, and painted illustrations for children's books. She was good—because she had a feel for the moment, the way children do? She lived in the moment, and without her I would not have enjoyed my last year of freedom as much as I did."

"Your last year of freedom?"

He nodded his head toward the man in the pale suit. "After a year he was standing again at the entrance to my property. I could have killed him—oh yes, I had got hold of weapons and learned to shoot and could hit a target with a telescopic sight from a great distance. But then someone else would have come. I thought, maybe the attaché is satisfied if I stand trial in Germany, and accepts the verdict, whichever way it goes. Perhaps after that there will be peace."

"You want to give yourself up?"

"That's why I'm flying to Germany. If it's possible, I'd prefer not to be arrested as soon as I reach Passport Control at the airport. I would like to see my mother first and talk to my defense attorney. Things go better if you go to the judge with your attorney and give yourself up than if you are arrested and taken before him by the police. I don't yet know how—" He turned to me with his quiet, gentle smile. "Will you lend me your passport? We look sufficiently like each other. You can say your wallet was stolen and you'll be given a little trouble, but it won't be serious. What's serious when your wallet gets stolen is that you have to replace everything in it, and you mustn't worry about that. After a few days you'll get your wallet back in the mail."

I just looked at him.

"Was that a little sudden? Sorry. Why don't we both take a nap?" He looked around. "There's an armchair still free over there by the window and another near the coat check—you'll understand if I leave the one by the window to you and take the other for myself?" He stood up. "Good night. Thank you for listening." He picked up his suitcase from where it stood by the bar, took his coat and hat from the coat check, sat down, rested his legs on the suitcase, covered himself with his coat, and pulled his hat down over his face.

11

I went to the window. It was bright daylight outside. The sun had come up red and was now yellow as it hung in the white sky. I have an old dream of going to St. Petersburg in the summer for the white nights. And now I had my white night here. But instead of water, bridges, strolling people, and loving couples, I was looking at empty runways, dark telescoping gates, and concrete buildings. Not a plane, not a car, not a human being was moving.

Quiet had descended on the lounge. Nobody was watching TV or drinking at the bar or talking. Some had opened their computers, others a book. Many were trying to sleep; people had even stretched themselves out on the floor. I went to the counter at the entrance and asked about the onward flight. The young woman had heard that a plane was being readied in Frankfurt. It wouldn't arrive before eight a.m., so there were at least another four hours before we would leave again.

I went back, pulled the empty armchair out of the light of the window and into the shadow of the wall, and sat down. In this position the man in the pale suit could no longer see me. Before, he had fixed his eyes on me every time I looked at him.

I think it's time I introduced myself. My name is Jakob Saltin, I studied physics, my specialty is traffic patterns, and I'm the head of the Institute for Traffic Studies at the University of Darmstadt. How many trains need how many tracks, how many cars need how many lanes? What causes traffic jams and how can they be prevented? Where must there be traffic lights and where must there not be? How should they be sequenced for optimal function? It is a fascinating branch of science. But it is as sober as all science is, as am I.

I no longer read any literary books—when would I find the time? But I read a story years ago in which a traveler tells another traveler that he's killed his wife. She had a lover—did he kill him too? At any rate he acted out of passion and despair, after music and alcohol had gone to his head. I'm not so sure about the alcohol, but the music definitely. If I remember correctly, the one traveler only listened to the other traveler. The other traveler didn't make any request of him.

My seatmate had tried his story out on me. Next he was going to have to tell the police, the prosecutor, and the judge, and he wanted to gauge how it would go over. What kind of a figure he cut in it. What he should leave out and what he should embellish. Had he selected me to listen precisely because I resembled him somewhat in face, body, and age? Had he intended to ask for my passport from the start? And to leave me so moved that I'd be unable to say no to him?

But no, the flight was fully booked; he couldn't have chosen the seat himself, so he couldn't have chosen me as his audience, either. Why was I so suspicious? The Russian mafia wasn't his world, he'd said—diplomatic receptions in Berlin, picnics in the desert in Kuwait, expensive houses on the coasts of Africa and America, and speculations with women, camels, and millions aren't my world, either. He didn't know how often he'd flown around the world—I had never yet flown around it and would not have been sitting in first class if business class hadn't been overbooked and I'd been given an upgrade. I have no sense whatever about the world my seatmate had described to me. Did I have any sense about my seatmate? Had he murdered his girlfriend?

For traffic scientists, accidents are parameters like any others. I'm not a cynic, but I'm also not sentimental. I know that accidents also happen to the human genus. There are human beings animated only by the desire for quick money and an easy life. I know them as students and as colleagues, in the business world and in politics. No, my seatmate wasn't one of them. He wasn't seeking the easy life, he was seeking the beautiful life. He wasn't driven by a lust for money, he wanted to play with it.

Or was there no difference between the two? The hard thing in life is to know when to hold fast to one's principles and when it's acceptable to bend them a little this way or that. I know that dividing line in my own profession. But outside it?

Then I fell asleep. It wasn't a deep sleep; I heard when a suitcase fell over, when a cell phone rang loudly, and when someone's voice rose. At seven thirty the loudspeaker informed us that a plane would land within an hour to take us to Frankfurt. Breakfast would be served at the buffet.

My seatmate came over. "Shall we?" We went to the buffet, collected coffee and tea, croissants and yoghurt, and sat down at a table. "Did you manage to sleep?" We had a polite conversation about sleeping on journeys and the quality of airplane seats and armchairs in lounges.

When we were called to board, we went together. People were moving in the passageways, the shops had opened, and arrivals and departures were being announced on the monitors and by the public address system. The airport had awakened.

12

We sat together on the flight from Reykjavik to Frankfurt as well. We didn't talk much anymore. He asked me about my wife and children. I'm taciturn when it comes to my wife, who's dead, and my daughter, who left—that my wife might still be alive and my daughter still with me if I'd given more of myself to both of them—how could I talk about that? Perhaps it isn't even true and I reproach myself unnecessarily.

I waited to see if he would actually ask for my passport again. I don't really like being drawn into other people's personal problems. I have enough to do solving traffic problems. They require my total attention, and that attention is rewarded; if they were solved, the world would be a better place. I'm proud that I developed a traffic blueprint for Mexico City that unblocked the traffic that used to clog it day after day and got it moving again and brought new oxygen to the suffocating city. Or could have, if the politicians had implemented the blueprint correctly.

But my seatmate was no longer a stranger. I had sat in the dark with him, emptied a bottle of pinot noir with him, listened to his story, seen him animated and moved and upset, squeezed his hand and put my hand on his back. I decided I would give him my passport.

But he didn't come back to his request, and I'm not someone to put myself forward. We were sitting in the last row in the upper deck, and when the plane reached its parking place at the gate in Frankfurt, we were the first downstairs and the first at the door. When the signal was given to open the door, he hugged me. I don't go in for today's all-hugging-all-kissing culture, but I returned his hug; two men had met, two strangers in the night, had talked, hadn't given each other everything they might have given, but had achieved a certain closeness. Perhaps I also returned the hug with real feeling because I'd been drinking champagne and was a little buzzed.

Then the door was opened and my seatmate didn't wheel his suitcase, he picked it up and ran. Once inside the terminal building I didn't see him again. Nor did I see him at Passport Control. He was gone.

13

With my passport. When I reached for my wallet in Passport Control, it wasn't there. My wallet belongs in my left inside pocket, and when it isn't there, it isn't there. I know where my things are.

During the flight my jacket, like his, had been in the charge of the stewardess; my seatmate must have asked her for his jacket at some point but given her my seat number, been handed my jacket, and taken the wallet out of it. He didn't want to risk my turning down his request.

The police were friendly. I told them that I'd shown my passport in New York and hadn't used it since. That I had no idea where I could have lost my wallet or where anyone could have stolen it from me. A policeman accompanied me back to the plane, which passengers were still exiting, and I hunted fruitlessly for my wallet around the seat, in the overhead locker, and in the coat cupboard. Then I was asked to go to the police station. Luckily my photograph is on the university Web site and there was someone in the dean's office; they confirmed it really was me.

I took a taxi. Only when we'd reached Darmstadt but were not yet at my house did I realize that the only money I had with me was what I was carrying loose in my pocket, far too little for the long journey. I told the driver and also said I had plenty of money in the house. But he didn't trust me, took what I had, and threw me out of the taxi with a lot of wailing and cursing.

It was very warm, but not sticky. After the night and the morning in planes and lounges, the police station, and the taxi, the air was invigorating, even though it was just Darmstadt city air that smelled of gasoline at the red light and of hot fat in front of the Turkish snack bar. I felt better with every step, buoyed up by the feeling that I'd accomplished something. What? I couldn't say. But it didn't matter.

What I couldn't say, nobody wanted to know anyway. Things would have been different if my wife had been waiting for me at home or if I knew that my daughter would be calling in the evening to welcome me back and ask about everything I'd done on my trip.

I reached home in the early afternoon. My little house has a little garden. I opened a deck chair and lay down. Then I stood up again and fetched a bottle of wine and a glass. I drank and fell asleep and woke up again, still with the good feeling that I'd achieved something. I pictured my seatmate going through Passport Control with my passport, ringing his mother's doorbell, embracing her, sharing a cup of tea, talking to his defense attorney, and going to the judge.

14

The next morning my life resumed again. In the last weeks of the semester there's an extra amount to do; over and above the classes and seminars and meetings there are the exams, plus on top of all that I had to catch up on everything I'd set aside because of the conference in New York. I had no time to think about my seatmate and his story. Yes, he was an interesting oddball and his story was an interesting story, but the whole thing was the affair of a single night, a night considerably shortened by the loss of six hours on the flight from west to east, then somewhat extended again by the stop in Reykjavik, but all in all a truncated night.

After a week my wallet came in the mail. I wasn't surprised, I had been relying on my seatmate. But I was relieved; I had been in need of my debit card and my credit cards from time to time.

The note that my seatmate had stuck in the left inside pocket of my jacket I found only weeks later. "I would rather not have taken your wallet. You were a wonderful traveling companion. But I need your wallet and you don't need the problem of deciding whether to say yes or no to me. Would you like to visit me in prison?"

The newspapers had already reported that he had surrendered and that the trial would soon resume. When they covered the trial, they also mentioned the old lady who claimed she had seen my seatmate not just push his girlfriend but force her over the balcony railing. She didn't appear before the court; a few days before my seatmate had given himself up, she'd disappeared. But her statement to the police was read out. I would have thought that a statement taken down and made watertight by the police would be more dangerous to the defendant than a statement in court that the defense attorney could pick apart. But the opposite turns out to be the case. It is harder to take apart a witness than to accuse a policeman of failing to ask this or that, thus getting a sworn statement that is one-sided and worthless.

She had disappeared a few days before my seatmate gave himself up. It didn't sit well with me. Had he—No, I couldn't imagine it. There are so many reasons why an old person can suddenly disappear. They can go too near the edge of a gully while out on a walk, and fall in. They can walk too far and lie down exhausted, they can have a heart attack in their holiday apartment and not be found for months or years. Such things keep happening.

My seatmate got eight years—some commentators felt this was too high and some too few. The court didn't absolve him of negligent homicide but nor did they convict him of murder; they convicted him of manslaughter in the heat of an agonizing, already long-standing dispute that suddenly came to a head.

I don't want to get into it. My professional specialty is traffic, not criminal law. I judge how the traffic in a city can be rescued from a coronary. Guilt is decided by judges who do nothing else, day in, day out.

But the verdict didn't convince me. There is a rightness when someone who has taken a life gives up his own. To lock him up for the rest of his days makes no sense. What does life in a cell have to do with a life that has been extinguished? Because there are mistaken verdicts there should be no death penalty, I know that. But eight years? The punishment was laughable. Anyone who hands down a sentence like that doesn't trust his own judgment. Anyone who hands down a sentence like that would do better to let the defendant go free.

I thought about visiting my seatmate in prison. But I find visits to people in the hospital hard enough. If I feel sorry for the patient, I can't find the right words to say, and if I don't feel sorry for the patient, I can't find any words at all. Get better soon—that's never misplaced. But what do you say to a prisoner?

15

Five years later he was at my front door. It was summer again, a warm late afternoon. I took his bag, led him into the garden, opened two deck chairs, and fetched two glasses of lemonade.

"When did you get out?"

He stretched. "It's so beautiful here! The trees, the flowers, the smell of new-mown grass, the birdsong. Do you mow the grass yourself? And were you the one who planted the hydrangeas? I've heard the color of hydrangeas changes according to the minerals in the soil. Isn't it amazing that your blue and pink hydrangeas are growing so close to each other? When did I get out? Yesterday. My last years got commuted to probation under certain conditions, but none of them prevents me from flying to America for a few days to draw on my cash." He smiled. "You're sort of on my way to America."

I looked at him. I could see no traces of the last years on his face. His hair was gray, but didn't make him look older, just better. He talked as pleasantly, moved as easily, and sat as comfortably as he had back then.

"Was it bad?"

He smiled again, and his smile was also as quiet and gentle

as it had been before. "I brought the library up to date and read all the things I'd always wanted to read and did a lot of sport. I did some deals with people I would rather not have done deals with, but don't we always have to do that in society?"

"What about the man in the pale suit?"

"He wasn't outside the prison yesterday. I hope enough is enough." He took a deep breath. "You know that when I borrow something, I return it. Can you help me? It's hard to save money in prison, and I don't know who else to ask for the money for the flight. My mother died right after the trial."

"The old lady who saw you . . ." The words came out just like that. Then I didn't know how to go on.

He laughed. "Would she lend me the money? I doubt it. And didn't she disappear back then?"

"Did you . . ." Again, I didn't know how to go on.

"Did I kill the incriminating witness?" He looked at me with friendly, forbearing mockery. "Why do you think so badly of me? Why is your first thought murder, and not that I used my money to buy the old lady off? That she didn't disappear into the grave with it, but to the Balearics or the Canaries?" He shook his head. "Do you think you could have prevented the murder? That you should have prevented it? You're right, once a murder has happened, questions arise." He was still looking mocking. "But if one did happen, I can't tell you. I have to tell you that it didn't. You see—we're at an impasse."

We were indeed at an impasse. "How much money do you need?"

"Five thousand euros."

I must have looked astonished, because he laughed and explained: "You will understand, I'm too old to fly toilet class and sleep in youth hostels."

"I can write you a check." I stood up.

"Could you give it to me in cash? I don't know if anyone will pay out that amount of money to me without further ado."

It was almost six o'clock and the banks were closed. But I could get the money together by using my debit card and my credit cards. "Then let's go."

"There's no hurry. I was actually wondering if perhaps I could impose on your hospitality for a few days . . ."

He was hoping I wouldn't let him finish the sentence. That I would be delighted to invite him to be my guest for a few days. And why not? It's true that I dislike any kind of disorder in my house. But I have a guest room and a guest bathroom, and whatever disorder my guests introduce is rectified by the cleaning lady and I don't notice it. I like it when I have someone I can share a glass with in the evenings and talk; it's better than sitting on my own. But I didn't respond right away.

"We would have a couple of nice days together. But unfortunately it won't work. I have to leave, the sooner the better. Do you think you could take me to the airport?"

I drove him to the airport, withdrew five thousand euros from various cash machines, and gave them to him. We said goodbye, but with a handshake this time, not a hug. Should I invite him to visit me again? I couldn't make up my mind in time. "Hope all goes well!"

He smiled, nodded, and went.

16

I looked after him until he disappeared into the hurly-burly. Then I left the airport and crossed the road to the parking garage, where I took the elevator up to the roof. I didn't find my car right away, and when I did find it, I couldn't feel the key in my pocket. The sky had clouded over and a cold wind was blowing. I stopped hunting and stood looking at the other parking garages, the hotels, the airport, and the planes taking off and landing. My seatmate would soon be sitting in one of the planes as it rose from the runway.

That was the end of our encounter. When we said goodbye the first time, I hadn't given any thought to whether we would see each other again. This time, I knew we wouldn't. Would I find a letter with a check in my mail one day?

I was freezing. What had seemed so good when he was with me suddenly felt not good; what had felt so close and warm suddenly felt strange and cold. That I had listened to his story, sharing his hopes and fears. That I would have given him my passport if he hadn't taken it, and my guest room if he hadn't decided to fly. That I had been glad he had tricked the police when he arrived, and was able to visit his mother and consult with his defense attorney. That I had believed against all reason that the death of his girlfriend was an accident and the disappearance of the old lady a riddle.

What had I done? Why had I got involved with him? Allowed myself to be used by him? Just because he had a quiet, gentle smile, a pleasant manner, and a softly cut, softly creased suit? What was the matter with me? Where did I leave my rational self, that makes me an alert observer and a clear thinker and a good scientist and that I'm proud of? Normally, I'm a good judge of people. I admit I had illusions about my wife at first. But I soon realized there was nothing behind her pretty face and her nice manner, no thought, no strength, no character. And sweet as I found my daughter and much as I loved her, I still realized immediately, as she grew up, that all she wanted was to have things, and showed no commitment to anything and achieved nothing.

No, letting myself get caught up with this person was incomprehensible.

And that it took me so long till I finally—Had I finally only regained my senses because a cold wind was blowing? If it had stayed warm, would I still be . . . ?

I watched a plane climb, a jumbo jet from Lufthansa. En route to America? Perhaps he'd gotten his ticket quickly and already caught this plane. Was he irritated to be sitting not in first class but in business?

The setting sun broke through the clouds for a moment, making the plane glisten, as if it were trying to turn into a fireball and blow itself apart. Nothing would remain of Werner Menzel or of my folly.

Then the sun disappeared behind the clouds, and the plane rose higher and higher in a curve, and then set its route. I found the key, got into the car, and drove home.

The Last Summer

1

He was remembering his first semester as a professor in New York. The pleasure it gave him when the invitation came, when the visa was stamped into his passport, when he boarded the plane in Frankfurt and reached JFK with his luggage in the warmth of the evening and took a taxi into the city. He had even enjoyed the flight, although the rows were tight together and the seats were narrow; as they crossed the Atlantic he saw another plane in the distance, and he felt as if he were sitting on the deck of a ship that encounters another ship in mid-ocean.

He had been in New York before as a tourist or visiting friends or as a guest at conferences. Now he lived according to the rhythms of the city. He belonged. He had his own apartment, like everyone; it was quite central, not far from the park and the river. Like everyone, he took the subway in the mornings, slid the card through the slot, went through the turnstile and down the steps to the platform, pushed his way into a car, couldn't move or turn the pages of his newspaper, and pushed his way out again twenty minutes later. In the evenings he managed to get a seat in the car, read the newspaper to the end, and did his shopping in the neighborhood. He could walk to the cinema and the opera.

He wasn't bothered by the fact that he wasn't an integral part of the university. His colleagues didn't have the same conversations with him they had with one another, and the students, who had him for only one semester, didn't take him as seriously as their professors whom they had to deal with from year to year. But his colleagues were friendly and the students alert, his class was a success, and from the window of his office he looked out onto a Gothic church built of red sandstone.

Yes, he had looked forward to the semester and later looked back on it with pleasure. But while he was actually there he was unhappy. His first semester in New York was the first semester in which he hadn't had to teach at his German university—and he would have liked to enjoy his freedom instead of teaching again. His apartment in New York was dark, and in the courtyard the sound of air conditioners was so loud that he had to use earplugs to be able to sleep. On the many evenings when he ate alone in cheap restaurants or watched bad movies, he felt lonely. In his office the air conditioning blew dry air into his face until his sinuses became infected and he had to have an operation. The operation was dreadful, and when he woke up from the anesthetic he found that he wasn't in a bed but on a gurney with other patients on gurneys and was sent home shortly afterward with a pounding head and a bleeding nose.

He hadn't admitted his unhappiness even to himself. He wanted to be happy, because he had made it from a little German university town to great New York and belonged there. He wanted to be happy because he had wanted this happiness so much and now it was here—or at least everything was here that he had always imagined it to consist of. Sometimes an inner voice raised itself to cast doubt on his happiness, but he silenced it. Even as a child, a schoolboy, and a student, he had struggled when he had to go on a trip and leave his world and his friends behind. How much he would have missed if he'd always stayed at home back then! So he told himself in New York it was his fate to have to overcome doubts in order to find happiness where it didn't seem at first to exist.

2

That summer an invitation to New York arrived again. He took the envelope out of the mailbox and opened it on the way to the bench where he always read his mail. The university in New York, which he'd been connected with for a quarter of a century now, was inviting him to organize a seminar next spring.

The bench was by the lake, on a part of the property that was separated from the rest and from the house by a small road. When they bought the house, his wife and children had been bothered by the road. They had got used to it. From the beginning he had liked it that there was a tiny kingdom to which he could open and close a door. When he came into his inheritance, he got the old boathouse fixed up and the roof built out. He had worked up there during many summers. But this summer he preferred to sit on the bench. It was his hiding place, invisible from the boathouse and the dock where his grandchildren liked to tumble around. If they swam out far enough, they saw him and he saw them, and they waved at one another.

He wouldn't teach next spring in New York. He would never teach in New York again. His life in New York, which over the years had become such a self-evident part of him that he had long since ceased asking himself whether he was happy there or not, was over. And because it was over, his thoughts went back to the first semester he'd spent there.

To admit to himself that he'd been unhappy in New York

back then would not be so bad if it didn't lead to the next admission. When he came back from New York, he was in an accident and got to know a woman; their bicycles collided when both of them were riding where they were not supposed to— he thought it was a charming way to meet someone. They dated for two years, going to the opera and the theater and to dinner, a few times they took trips together for a couple of days, and she regularly spent the night at his place or he at hers. He found her adequately beautiful and adequately clever, he liked holding her and being held by her, and he thought he'd finally arrived. But when she moved away because of her job, the relationship soon became labored and then died. Only now could he admit he'd been relieved. That he'd found the two years an effort. That he would often have been happier if he'd stayed home and read and listened to music instead of meeting her. He had met her because once again he thought all the components of happiness were there and he had to be happy.

How was it with the other women in his life? With his first love? He was happy when Barbara, the prettiest girl in the class, went to the movies with him, accepted his invitation to eat an ice cream, then let him take her home and kiss her at the door. He was fifteen; it was his first kiss. A few years later Helena took him to bed, and everything went fine the very first time, he didn't come too soon, and she came too, and all through the night he gave her what a man can give a woman, he the nineteen-year-old, she thirty-two. They were together until at thirty-five she married a lawyer in London to whom, as he eventually discovered, she'd been engaged for years. He took his exams, did better than he had expected, became an assistant professor, wrote essays and books, and became a full professor. He was happy—or did he just want to be happy because everything was going well? Because all the components of happiness were there. He had sometimes wondered if life were not elsewhere and then pushed the question away. Just as he had pushed away the fact that it was vanity that allowed him to court Barbara and serve Helena, and that he often found the effort in service of that vanity exhausting.

He shied away from any thoughts about happiness in his marriage and with his family.

He wanted to enjoy the blue sky and the blue lake and the green meadows and woods. He didn't love the landscape for the distant view of the Alps, he loved it for the gentle curve of the nearby mountains as they rose upward and the lake found its place among them. A girl and a boy were out there in the boat; he was rowing and she was dangling her legs in the water. The drops falling from the oars glittered in the sun, and the little waves set up by the boat and the girl's feet spread wide over the smooth surface of the water. The two children, it must be Meike, his son's eldest daughter, and David, his daughter's eldest son, weren't talking. Since the mailman's car had gone by, there had been nothing further to disturb the morning quiet. His wife was making breakfast in the house; a grandchild would come soon to fetch him inside.

Then he thought that he should take the insight about how deceptive his happiness had been not as negative, but as positive.

For someone who wants to take leave of life, what better insight could there be? He wanted to take his leave, because the last months that were ahead of him were going to be terrible. Not that he couldn't tolerate pain. But when the pain became unbearable, he would go.

But he didn't manage to take the insight as positive. The idea of summer together, his last summer, was the idea of a last shared happiness. It hadn't taken much persuasion for his two children and their families to come to the house on the lake for four weeks, but it had taken a little. He had also had to use a little persuasion on his wife; she would rather have gone to Norway with him, because that's where her grandmother came from and they'd never been. Now he had his family together, and his old friend was also coming to visit for a few days. He had thought he'd prepared their last shared happiness. Now he wondered if once again he had only collected the components of happiness.

3

"Grandfather!" He heard a child's voice and quick child's feet running across the road and the meadow to the lake. It was Matthias, his daughter's youngest son and the youngest of his five grandchildren, a sturdy five-year-old with a mop of blond hair and blue eyes. "Breakfast's ready!" When Matthias saw the boat with his brother and his cousin, he called out to them again and again and hopped to and fro on the deck till they tied up. "Shall we race?" The children broke into a run and he followed them slowly. A year ago he would have run with them, and a couple of years ago he would have won. But watching them race up the hill ahead of him and then seeing the older children hang back to let the little one win was better than doing it with them. Yes, this was how he had pictured their last summer together.

He had also pictured how he would go. A doctor who was a friend and colleague had obtained the cocktail that organizations for assisted suicide give their members. Cocktail—he liked the description. He had never had a taste for cocktails or ever tried one; his first would also be his last. He also liked the description "angel of death" for the member of the organization who brings the cocktail to the fellow member who is ready to die; he would be his own angel of death. When things were that far along, he would stand up without any fuss from the evening gathering in the living room, go out, drink the cocktail, wash out the bottle and put it away, and go back to join the others in the living room. He would listen, fall asleep, and die, they would leave him to sleep and find him dead the next morning, and the doctor would pronounce it to have been heart failure. A painless, peaceful death for him; a painless, peaceful farewell for the others.

Things weren't that far along yet. The table was laid in the dining room. At the beginning of the summer he had extended the table and imagined that he and his wife would sit at the head. Next to him their daughter and her husband, next to his wife their son and his wife, with the five grandsons and grand-daughters around the end. But the others didn't see anything appealing in this order and sat wherever it suited them. Today the only free seat was between his daughter-in-law and her six-year-old son, Ferdinand, who was clearly in a sulk and had pulled away from his mother. "What's the matter?" But Ferdinand shook his head wordlessly.

He loved his children, their spouses, and his grandchildren. He liked having them around him, liked their bustle, their talk, and their games, even their noise and their arguments. What he liked best was to sit in a corner of the sofa, lost in his own thoughts, amid them all and yet self-contained. He also liked working in libraries and cafés; he found it easy to concentrate while surrounded by the rustle of paper and conversation and movement. Sometimes he joined the others in a game of bowls, sometimes he accompanied them on the flute when they made music, sometimes he dropped a remark into their conversations. They would be surprised, as he himself was to find himself part of their games or their music or their talk.

He also loved his wife. "Of course I love my wife," he would have said if anyone had asked him. It was wonderful when he was sitting in the corner of the sofa and she came and sat next to him. It was even more wonderful to watch her in the circle of the family. Among the young ones she herself became young, as if she were the student again from the first semester, whom he met just when he was taking his exams. She was without sophistication and without malice, she had none of the traits that were both desirable and repellent in Helena. He felt back then as if loving her purified him of the experience of using and being used that was the residue of his relationship with Helena. They got married when she too had completed her education and become a teacher. The two children came in quick succession, and his wife soon returned to teaching half-time. She did everything effortlessly: the children, school, the apartment in the city, and the house in the country, even occasionally a semester with him and the children in New York.

No, he told himself, he mustn't be afraid to think about his happiness in his marriage and with his family. It was real. Just as the first days of their shared summer had been real; his grandchildren were busy among themselves, his children and their spouses enjoyed time for its own sake, and his wife was happy working in the garden. Fourteen-year-old David was in love with thirteen-year-old Meike—he could see this, though the others seemed not to. The weather was beautiful day after day, weather fit for a king, his wife said with a smile, and the thunderstorm on their second evening was fit for a king too; he sat out on the veranda and was overwhelmed by the blackness of the clouds, the lightning and thunder, and finally the liberating downpour.

Even if what he had collected once again was no more than the components of happiness, even if the happiness of this last shared summer concealed a misfortune—so what? He wouldn't be around to experience it.

4

When night came and they were in bed, he asked his wife, "Were you happy with me?"

"I'm glad we're here. We couldn't have been happier if we'd gone to Norway."

"No, I mean, were you happy with me?"

She sat up and looked at him. "All the years we've been married?"

"Yes."

She lay down again. "I didn't like it that you were away so often. That I was alone a lot. And that I had to raise the children on my own. When Dagmar ran away when she was fifteen and was gone for six months, you were there, I admit, but you were in such despair you retreated into yourself and I was alone again. When Helmut . . . but what am I talking about? You know yourself when things were fine with me and when they weren't. I know the same about you. When the children were small and I had started teaching again, you got the short end of the stick. You would have liked me to play more of a role in your working life, like reading the things you wrote. You would also have liked to have sex more often." She turned onto her side with her back to him. "I would have liked to cuddle with you more often."

After a while he heard her quiet breathing. Did this mean there was nothing more to say?

His left hip hurt. The pain wasn't acute, but regular and constant and felt as if it wanted to become a permanent part of him. Or was it already a permanent part? Hadn't his left hip and his left leg been hurting for days, no, weeks when he climbed the stairs? Hadn't there been a long-standing weakness that he had to overcome with increasing effort and stabbing pain? He hadn't paid attention. Once he'd climbed the stairs, the weakness disappeared. But the stabbing pain that accompanied the climb could have heralded the pain he was feeling now, and it made him afraid. Hadn't the CT scan shown tumors spreading in his left hip?

He no longer remembered. He didn't want to be one of those sick people who know everything about their illness, who research on the Internet and in books and conversations and embarrass their doctors. Left hip, right hip—he hadn't been paying attention when the doctor told him which bones were already affected. He'd told himself he would notice soon enough.

He turned on his side too. Did his left hip still hurt? Or was it the right hip now? He listened to his insides, at the same time hearing the wind in the trees outside the open window and the croaking of the frogs by the lake. He saw stars up in the sky and thought, they're not golden and they're not resplendent, they're hard and cold like little distant neon bulbs.

His left hip was indeed still hurting. His right hip too. When he touched his legs, the pain was there, and also when he felt his spine and up into his neck and arms. Wherever he felt, the pain was waiting for him, saying, I live here now. This is my home.

5

He slept badly and was up with the sun. He tiptoed to the door, opened it cautiously, and closed it the same way. The floors, the stairs, the doors, everything creaked. He made tea in the kitchen and took the cup out onto the veranda. The sky was light, and the birds were singing.

Occasionally he helped his wife with cooking or laying the table or doing the dishes. He had never put a single meal on the table by himself. In earlier days, if his wife had to be away, breakfast went by the board and he took the children to a restaurant for lunch and supper. But in earlier days he had also had no time. Now he had time.

He found Dr. Oetker's cookbook for beginners in the kitchen and took it out to the veranda. With a cookbook even he, the philosopher with an expertise in analytical philosophy, had to be able to make pancakes for breakfast. Even he? Most specifically! "What can be described can also take place," as Wittgenstein teaches in the *Tractatus Logico-Philosophicus*.

At first he didn't find pancakes in the cookbook. Did pancakes have another name? What cannot be named, cannot be found. What cannot be found, cannot be cooked.

But then he found the recipe and calculated up the quantity of ingredients for eleven people. He set to work in the kitchen. It took him a long time to assemble 1⅓ pounds of flour, eleven eggs, 2⅓ pints of milk, a generous ¾ pint of mineral water, just under a pound of margarine, sugar, and salt. He was annoyed that there were no specific quantities for sugar, and salt. How was he supposed to divide sugar and salt by four and multiply by eleven? He was also annoyed that he found no instructions on how to separate the egg whites from the egg yolks and beat them stiff. He would like to have made the pancakes or egg pancakes soft and light. But he managed the sieving and the beating and the stirring without making any lumps.

As he took the pan out of the cupboard, it slipped from his hand and landed on the stone floor with a clatter. He picked it up and listened to the house. After a few seconds he heard his wife's steps on the stairs. She came into the kitchen in her nightshirt and looked around.

Now, he thought. He took her in his arms. She felt awkward. I probably feel awkward too, he thought. When did we last take each other in our arms? He held her close, and she didn't soften into his embrace but she did put her arms around him. "What are you doing in the kitchen?"

"Pancakes—I want to make a test one first. I'll cook the rest when everyone's at the breakfast table. I'm sorry I woke you."

She looked at the table, where there were still flour, eggs, and margarine, and the bowl with the batter. "You made that?"

"Do you want to try the test one?" He let go of his wife, turned on the stove, and set the pan on the flame, looked at the cookbook, heated margarine, poured a little batter into the pan, then took the half-cooked pancake out and put it on a plate, heated more margarine, flipped the pancake and put it back in the pan, and finally presented it all golden yellow to his wife.

She ate. "It tastes like a real pancake."

"It is a real pancake. Do I get a kiss?"

"A kiss?" She stared at him, astonished. How long is it, he wondered again, since we last kissed each other? She slowly put down the fork and the plate, came to him at the stove, gave him a kiss on the cheek, and stayed standing next to him, as if she didn't know what to do next.

Then Meike was standing in the door looking questioningly at her grandparents. "What's going on?"

"He's making pancakes."

"Grandfather's making pancakes?" She couldn't believe it. But there all the components were, the bowl with the batter, the pan, the half pancake on the plate, and Grandfather in an apron. Meike turned, ran up the stairs, and banged on the doors. "Grandfather's making pancakes!"

6

Today he didn't withdraw to the bench by the lake. He fetched a chair from the boathouse and sat down on the deck. He opened a book, but didn't read; he watched his grandchildren.

Yes, David was in love with Meike. The way he tried to impress her, the way he strove to be casual in every posture and every movement, the way he checked before he did a dive with a somersault and a flip to see if she was watching, the way he showed off about the books he'd read and the films he'd seen, the way he talked with superiority about his future. Did Meike not notice, or was she playing with David? She seemed unimpressed and quite natural, and paid no more attention to David or bestowed any more of her good mood on him than she did on the others.

The pains of first love! He saw David's uncertainty and felt once again the uncertainty he himself had been plagued by fifty years before. He too had wanted to be everything back then and sometimes he felt he was, and then again sometimes he felt as if he were nothing. Back then he too thought that if Barbara saw who he was and how he loved her, she would love him too, but he could neither show who he was nor tell her that he loved her. He too had sought to find a promise in every tiny gesture of attention and familiarity and yet still knew that Barbara was promising him nothing. He too took refuge in a heroic indifference in which he believed in nothing and hoped for nothing and needed nothing. Until longing overwhelmed him again.

He was seized by pity for his grandson—and for himself. The pains of first love, the pains of growing up, the disappointments of adult life—he would have liked to say something comforting or encouraging to David. What could be of help to him anyway? He stood up and went to sit down cross-legged with the two of them on the deck.

"Honestly, Grandfather, I would never have believed you and the pancakes."

"I had fun cooking. Will the two of you help me tomorrow? I don't want to get too cocky, but I should be able to manage spaghetti Bolognese and salad with your assistance."

"Chocolate mousse for dessert?"

"If it's in Dr. Oetker's cookbook for beginners."

Then they sat together in silence. He had interrupted their conversation, and didn't know how to get the three of them talking. "Then I'll go back. Tomorrow at eleven? Shopping first, then cooking?"

Meike laughed at him. "Cool, Grandfather, but we'll see each other again today."

He sat in his chair again. Matthias and Ferdinand had found a flat place in the lake a few yards from the shore, had dragged over all the stones they could find, and were building an island. He looked for David and Matthias's sister. "Where's Ariane?"

"On your bench."

He stood up again and walked to his bench. His left hip hurt. Ariane was reading with one foot on the bench and the book on her knee; she heard him coming and looked up. "Is it okay for me to sit here?"

"Of course. Can I come and sit with you?"

She took her foot off the bench, closed the book, and slid sideways. She saw him reading the title: *The Postman Always*

Rings Twice. "It was in your bookcase. Maybe it's not for me, but it's gripping. I thought we'd be doing more stuff together. But David's only got eyes for Meike, and Meike only has eyes for David, even if she's pretending it's not the case, and he doesn't notice."

"Are you sure?"

Her look was as precocious as it was pitying, and she nodded. She will be a beautiful woman, he thought, and imagined her taking off her glasses one day, shaking her hair loose, and pouting. "So that's what's with David and Meike. Shall the two of us do something together?"

"What?"

"We could go look at churches and castles, or we could visit a painter I know, or a car mechanic who's got a workshop that looks exactly the way it did fifty years ago."

She thought. Then she stood up. "Good, let's go visit the painter."

7

After a week his wife asked, "What's going on? If this summer's right, every previous summer was wrong, and if every previous summer was right, this one's not. You're not reading anymore and you aren't writing. All you do is go around with the grandchildren or your children, and yesterday you came into the garden and wanted to clip the hedge. Any time there's an opportunity to grab me, you grab me. Really, it's as if you can't keep your hands off me. I'm not saying you can't grab me. You can . . ." She blushed and shook her head. "Anyhow, things aren't the same and I want to know why."

They were sitting on the veranda. Their children and spouses were spending the evening with friends, and the grandchildren were in bed. He had lit a candle, opened a bottle of wine, and poured glasses for the two of them.

"Wine by candlelight—that's a first too."

"Isn't it time for me to start—that and the grandchildren and the children and the hedge? And for me to know how good you feel again?" He put his arm around her.

But she shook him off. "No, Thomas Wellmer. It's not okay. I'm not a machine you can switch off and switch on. I had imagined our marriage differently, but that's apparently not how it went, and so I came to terms with the way it actually was. I'm not going to get caught up in a particular mood, in a single summer that's over after a few weeks. I'd rather cut my hedge myself."

"I retired three years ago. I'm sorry it took me so long to realize about the freedom that retirement brings. Retirement from a university isn't as complete as it would be from a business; there are still doctoral students and a seminar here and a seat on a commission there, and you think now's the time to do the writing you always wanted to do and never had the time for before. It's like switching off the engine and your car keeps rolling in neutral. If the road then slopes a bit . . ."

"You're the car, and retirement has switched off your engine. But who's the slope?"

"Everyone who's still behaving as if the engine were still running."

"So I have to give you special treatment. Not the way I would if the engine were still running, but as if it were off. Then . . ."

"No, you don't have to do anything. After three years the car's stopped."

". . . so from now on you take care of the grandchildren and trim the hedge?"

He laughed. "And never take my hands off you."

They sat side by side and he could feel her skepticism. He felt it in her shoulder, her arm, her hip, her thigh. If he put his arm around her again, maybe she wouldn't shake it off—they'd talked and listened to each other. But she would wait for him to remove it. Or would she lay her head on his shoulder after a while? The way she'd put her arm around him while he was making the pancakes, not in agreement, not as a promise, but just like that.

8

He courted her. In the mornings, he brought her tea in bed; when she was working in the garden, he brought her lemonade; he trimmed the hedge and mowed the lawn; he made it a rule to cook in the evenings, mostly assisted by Ariane; he was there for the grandchildren when they were bored; he made sure the supplies of apple juice, mineral water, and milk didn't run out. Every day he invited his wife to go for a walk, just the two of them, and at first she wanted to get back to the house and her tasks as quickly as possible, but then she let him extend the distances and sometimes hold her hand—until she needed it to lift something or pluck it and examine it. One evening he drove her to the restaurant on the far side of the lake; it had one star, and dinner was served in the meadow under fruit trees. They looked out at the water glinting like molten metal in the evening sun, lead perhaps with a tinge of bronze, smooth, until two swans came in to land, their wings flapping noisily.

He put his left hand on the table. "You know that swans . . ."

"I know." She lay her hand on his.

"I'd like to make love to you when we get home."

She didn't pull her hand away. "Do you know when the last time was that we made love?"

"Before your operation?"

"No, after that. You told me I'm as beautiful as I was before and you love the new breast as much as you loved the old one. But then I had to take a bath and I saw the red scar and I knew it wasn't okay and everything was just an effort, I made an effort and you made an effort. You were very understanding and very considerate, and said you didn't want to pressure me, and I should give you a signal when things were better. But when I didn't give you a signal, that was fine with you too, and you didn't give me one, either. Then I realized it had been the same way before the operation and nothing happened back then, either, unless I was the one to give a signal. I didn't want to give any more signals."

He nodded. "Lost years—I can't tell you how sorry I am. Back then I thought I had to prove to myself and everyone else that I could become rector of the university or get into politics, and because you didn't take part in any of that I felt you'd betrayed me. But you were right. I look back on those years and they were pointless. All they were was noisy and rushed."

"Did you have a lover?"

"Oh, no. I never let anyone or anything near me outside work. I'd never have got anything done otherwise."

She laughed softly. Because she was remembering his craze for work back then? Because she was relieved he'd had no lover?

He asked for the check.

"Do you think we still can?"

"I'm as anxious as I was the first time. Maybe more anxious. I don't know how it will be."

9

It wasn't. Pain struck in the middle of things, exploding in his coccyx and sending waves into his back and his hips and thighs. It was worse than the worst pain he'd had thus far. It annihilated his desire, his sensations, his mind, and made him its creature, unable to escape its grip or even to long for it to stop. Without intending to or even being aware of it, he groaned aloud.

"What is it?"

He rolled onto his back and pressed both hands against his forehead. What should he say? "I have sciatica like I've never had." He struggled to his feet. In the bathroom he swallowed some of the Oxycontin the doctor had prescribed for crises. He propped his arms on the sink and looked into the mirror. Although he felt different from any way he'd felt in his life, his face was the same as usual. His dark blond hair with streaks of gray and gray sideburns, his gray-green eyes, the deep creases around his nose and from his nose to his mouth, the tiny hairs in his nostrils that he would trim tomorrow, his thin lips—it did him good to share the pain with this familiar face and to reassure it and himself with an obstinate expression that there was life in the old dog yet. When the pain eased, he went back into the bedroom.

His wife had fallen asleep. He sat down on the edge of the bed, careful not to wake her. Her eyelids trembled. Was she half asleep and half awake? Was she dreaming? What was she dreaming? He knew her face so well. The young face that lived within it, and the old one. The childlike, happy, innocent one, and the tired, bitter one. How did the two faces coexist?

He stayed sitting there, not wanting to provoke the pain. It had shown him that it was not only at home in his body, but that it now ruled the house. For now it had retreated into a back room, but left the doors open in order to be right there if insufficient respect was shown.

He was touched by his wife's hair. Dyed brown, with the gray and the white growing back through it—the battle against age, fought again and again, lost but never abandoned. If his wife didn't dye her hair, with her aquiline nose, high cheekbones, deep eyes and lines, she'd look like a wise old Indian woman. He had never worked out if her eyes were sometimes unfathomable because her feelings and thoughts were so profound, or because they were so empty. He would never work it out now.

She apologized the next morning. "I'm sorry. The champagne, the wine, the food, the sex, your sciatica just when it was getting good—it was all a little much. I just went to sleep."

"No, I'm the one who should be sorry. The doctor told me that I had to expect sciatica and take pills if I had an attack. I had no idea it would be so strong, and come at exactly the wrong moment." He was afraid of turning on his side, and stretched out his arm.

She laid her head on his shoulder. "I have to make breakfast."

"No, you don't have to."

"Yes, I do."

She was only playing. She wanted what he wanted too. He begged the pain to stay in the back room, at least for this morning, at least for an hour. "Will you sit on me?"

10

When they came downstairs, the others had almost finished breakfast. Ariane looked at her grandparents as if she knew why they were late. Twelve-year-old Ariane? But he went red, as did his wife. Then, as if to show the clique that she and he had been having a thing together, she gave him a kiss.

Around midday he went to the station to collect his old friend. The train pulled in and stopped, and because either the cars were too high for the platform or the platform was too low for the car, his friend had to take a small jump, which he did with a resigned smile, as if convinced he was going to fall and instead of a short visit with an old friend he would be facing a long stay in a provincial hospital.

Resigned, as if to a game that was lost before it even began, while also in high spirits, because that's how things were but they just didn't matter—this was the essence of his charm. That's how he had been as a student, without great effort or arrogance, friendly toward everyone, loved by everyone, even by those who were his examiners and later by his employers. He became a successful lawyer whose success derived partly from his professional knowledge and partly from his manner with clients, opposing counsel, and judges. He charmed them. He also charmed the wives and children of his friends; they loved him, although even among his friends one or another had married a woman who wanted her husband for herself, regardless of his old friends.

His son, Helmut, was particularly fond of this friend; when he was a child, he had sometimes gone on vacation with him and his father: male vacations. In the winter they went skiing, and when Helmut had had enough or couldn't go on anymore, the friend, who hurtled down the slopes in jeans and an over-coat, would put him between his legs.

For the little boy, the friend with his billowing dark coat who bore him safely and swiftly down the valley was a hero like Batman. Later on he advised him in his studies and his career; without him Helmut would not have decided to become a lawyer himself. He would have liked to have come along to the station too, but the trips from the station to the house and then back again the next evening were the only opportunity the friends would have to be alone together.

Along the way they talked about retirement, their families, the summer. Then his friend asked, "What's the cancer doing?"

"Let's stop up there"—he pointed to the mountain ahead of them on the road—"and walk a little." He had asked himself again and again if he should tell his friend about what he'd decided. They had no other secrets from each other, and had been able to talk that much more easily about the cancer because they both faced the same fate; both had been diagnosed years before, with different forms of it, which would take different courses, but both had been treated with an operation followed by radiation and chemotherapy. But knowing of his intentions, how would his friend manage to face the family?

They went up over the peak. To the right was the beginning of the woods, to the left they had the view of the lake, the mountains, and in the distance the Alps. It was warm, the soft heavy warmth of summer.

"It's only a matter of time before the bones give out and they crumble and break and the pain becomes unbearable. Sometimes I get a foretaste, but things are still okay. What's yours doing?"

"It's in remission, has been for the last four years. Last month was supposed to be time for my checkup, and for the first time I just didn't go." The friend raised his hands fatalistically and let them fall. "What do you do when the pain becomes unbearable?"

"What would you do?"

They walked for a long time and the friend didn't answer. Then he laughed. "Enjoy the summer as long as it lasts. What else?"

11

After dinner he sat in the corner of the sofa and observed the others. They were playing a game that could be played by a maximum of eight people. Without anyone noticing he could keep changing his position and moving the cushions behind his back, then against his hips, then under his thighs. Each change brought relief until pain asserted itself in the new position as it had in the old. He had taken Oxycontin but it didn't help anymore. What now? Should he drive into the city and ask his doctor for morphine? Or had the time come to take the bottle out of the wine refrigerator, where it was hidden behind a half bottle of champagne, and drink the cocktail?

When he had imagined his last evening, he had imagined it as being pain free. Now he realized it wasn't simple to decide on the right evening. The longer it went on and the worse he got, the less often there would be pain-free evenings, and the more welcome and indispensable they would be. How could he relinquish such an evening to death? On the other hand he didn't want to go in pain. Was morphine the solution? Would it save the pain-free evenings from being indispensable rarities and allow them to become plausible opportunities?

The doors and windows stood open, and the mild breeze brought mosquitoes from the lake. When he tried to hit the mosquito on his left arm with his right hand, he couldn't lift it. The hand would not obey him. When he shifted position things were okay again, and they were still okay when he sat the way he'd been sitting before and his hand wouldn't obey him. He tried out different positions, and he could lift his hand in each of them, so that finally he wondered if he'd imagined its failure. But he knew better, and he also knew that once again something had happened from which there was no going back.

The game came to an end, and his friend told stories about his cases. In earlier days his children had never been able to get enough of them, and now his grandchildren couldn't, either. It made him ashamed. What had he had that he could tell his children? What did he have to tell his grandchildren? That Kant was a good billiards player and earned money for his studies that way, that Hegel and his wife imitated the family life of Martin Luther and Katharina von Bora, that Schopenhauer behaved disgustingly to his mother and his sister, and that Wittgenstein was touchingly protective of his sister—he knew a few anecdotes about philosophers and a few anecdotes from history that his grandfather had told him. Out of his own work there were no stories he could tell—what did that say about him? And about his work? And about analytical philosophy? Was it nothing more than an elaborate waste of human intelligence?

Then his friend yielded to his family's requests and sat down at the piano. He smiled at him and played the Chaconne from the Partita in D Minor, which they had heard Menuhin play when they were students and learned to love. A transcription for piano—he hadn't known that it existed and that his friend could play it. Had he practiced it for him? Was it his farewell present? The music and his friend's gift of it moved him to tears, which kept on coming even when his friend switched to jazz—which was what his children and grandchildren actually wanted to hear.

His wife noticed, came and sat beside him, and laid her head on his shoulder. "I'm going to cry too. The day began so beautifully and is ending so beautifully too."

"Yes."

"Shall we stand up and go upstairs? If the others notice we're no longer here, they'll understand."

12

Then it was halftime. He knew the second half of their shared summer would pass more quickly than the first—and the first had passed in a flash. He thought about what more he could tell the children. Dagmar—that she shouldn't be so concerned about her children? That she was a good biologist and should go on working rather than squander her gift? That she was spoiling her husband and it wasn't doing either of them any good? Helmut—did it really interest him which company merged with which and which company took over which? Did it really interest him to make the piles of money he was making? Did he not wish that with the example of his father's friend in front of his eyes, he'd become another kind of lawyer than the one he was now?

He couldn't talk to them. Dagmar had gone and married a self-important idiot and he could only hope she wouldn't notice and would continue to be dazzled by his wealth and his good manners. Helmut had discovered a taste for money and become greedy for it, and his wife enjoyed the fruits of it. Perhaps both children had embarked on a life of externals out of insecurity, and perhaps he had failed to give them that sufficient security. And now he could no longer give them more. He could tell them that he loved them. If parents and children in American movies could say such things to one another with ease, then he could too.

No matter what wasn't okay with his children—this summer they were undemanding, good-natured, and affectionate. He wouldn't be taking such delight in his grandchildren if his children weren't doing something right. No, he couldn't give the children any pointers. He could only tell them that he loved them.

One day the pain was so fierce that he took a train into the city and asked his doctor for morphine. The doctor, after some hesitation, gave him a prescription, along with copious instructions as to dosage and effect. The lady in the pharmacy was friendlier than the doctor; he had been a customer for years and she handed him the box with a glass of water and a sad smile. "So it's that far along."

He missed the afternoon train and took the one in the evening. He had left his car at the station, wondered if he was fit to drive but hadn't been warned otherwise, and got home safely after a journey along empty roads. The house lay in darkness. If everyone was already asleep, he was in no hurry. He could go and sit on the bench by the lake and enjoy this evening, with the pain not just having retreated into a back room but being safely locked in.

Yes, morphine was the answer. A pain-free evening was no longer an indisputable rarity, but an achievable opportunity. He felt light; it wasn't just that his body didn't hurt, it was pulsating steadily and gently, supporting him, carrying him, on wings. Without moving he could reach for the lights on the far side of the lake and even grasp the stars.

13

He heard footsteps and recognized them as his wife's. He slid along to one side of the bench so that she had room on the other. "You heard the car?"

She sat down without replying. When he tried to put an arm around her shoulders, she bent forward so that the gesture landed in empty air. She held up the bottle with the cocktail and said, "Is this what I think it is?"

"What do you think it is?"

"Don't play games with me, Thomas Wellmer. What is it?"

"It's a particularly powerful pain medication that has to be stored at a cold temperature and mustn't fall into the grandchildren's hands."

"That's why you hid it behind the champagne bottle in the wine refrigerator?"

"Yes. I don't understand what you—"

"I'm having particularly bad pains. I've had them since I found this while preparing a dish with champagne for the two of us. So why don't I drink the whole thing?" She unscrewed the cap and raised the bottle to her lips.

"Don't do that."

She nodded. "One evening when we're sitting together and enjoying ourselves, you'll go out, drink the whole bottle, come back in, and go to sleep. Will you say to us first that you're really tired and you may nod off, and if you do, please will we leave you to sleep?"

"I haven't planned it that clearly."

"But you wanted to do it without telling me, without asking me or talking to me about it. That much you did plan. Am I right?"

He shrugged. "I don't know what's the matter with you. I wanted to go when the pain becomes unbearable. I wanted to go in a way that doesn't leave anyone else with a problem."

"Do you remember our wedding? Till death do us part? Not till you worm your way into death's affections and run off with him. And do you remember that I didn't want to get involved in the happiness of a single summer that's over in a matter of weeks? Did you think I wouldn't find out the truth?

Or that when I did, you'd be dead? And that then I'd be unable to get you to talk? You didn't have a lover, but the way you've betrayed me now is no better, in fact it's worse."

"I thought it wouldn't come out. I also thought it's a good way to say goodbye. What would you—"

"A good way to say goodbye? You go, and I don't know you're going? That's supposed to be a good way? It's no way to say goodbye, and it's definitely not one I'm going to accept. And you're not saying goodbye to me, you're saying goodbye to yourself, and you want me there to act as a sort of movie extra."

"I still don't understand why you're so upset . . ."

She got to her feet. "That's right, you don't understand what you're doing. I'll tell the children first thing tomorrow, and then I'm leaving. Do whatever you want here. I'm not going to stay here playing an extra, and I'd be amazed if the children stayed, either." She set the bottle down on the bench and left.

He shook his head. Something had gone wrong, he didn't know exactly what. But there was no doubt something hadn't gone the way it was supposed to. He'd have to talk to his wife tomorrow morning. He hadn't seen her that upset for a long time.

14

She wasn't in their bed when he went to lie down, nor when he got up. He made breakfast with his children and woke the grandchildren. When they were all at the table, she arrived. She didn't sit down.

"I'm driving to the city. In the course of the next few evenings your father intends to kill himself while surrounded by his loved ones. I only found out by accident; he didn't intend to say a word to me or to you, just drink the stuff and go to sleep and die. I don't want anything to do with it. He thought it up on his own, he can do it on his own."

Dagmar said to her husband, "Take the children and do something with them. Not just our children—all of them." She said it so firmly that her husband stood up and went, and the grandchildren went with him. Then she turned to her father. "You want to kill yourself? Like Mother said?"

"I thought everyone didn't have to know. Actually, nobody was to know. The pain's getting worse and when it becomes unendurable, I want to go. What's wrong with that?"

"What's wrong is that you didn't tell us and didn't want to tell us. And if not us children, then Mother. Whether the pain becomes unendurable also depends on what Mother helps you to bear. And I thought we too . . ." Dagmar looked at her father in disappointment.

Helmut stood up. "Leave it, Dagmar. This is for our parents to decide between themselves. I for one am not going to get into the middle of it, and you'd be wise not to, either."

"But they won't sort it out themselves. Mother said she wants nothing to do with it." Dagmar looked at her brother, confused.

"That's also a way of sorting it out." He turned to his wife. "Come on, we're going to pack and leave."

They went. Dagmar got to her feet hesitantly, gave her father and her mother a questioning look, received no answers, and left too. The house was filled with the bustle of cupboards and chests being emptied, books and games being collected, beds stripped, and suitcases packed. The parents told their children to fetch this and not to forget that, and because the children could feel that the world was off-kilter, they obeyed.

His wife had already packed during the night. She stood for

a while in the kitchen, just staring into space. Then she looked at him. "I'm going to drive now."

"You don't have to."

"Yes, I do."

"Are you driving to the city?"

"I don't know. I still have three weeks' holiday." She left, and he heard her saying goodbye to the children and grandchildren, opening and closing the front door, starting the car, and driving off. The others finished packing soon afterward. They came into the kitchen to say goodbye, the children awkwardly, the grandchildren troubled. He heard them leave the house too, slam car doors, and drive away. Then everything was still.

15

He stayed sitting, unable to believe how fast the house had emptied itself. He didn't know what to do. How he should spend the morning and the day, and the next day and the next week, whether he should kill himself right away or later. Finally he stood up and cleared the table, loaded the dirty dishes and cutlery into the dishwasher, added the detergent, switched on the machine, collected the sheets and towels upstairs, and carried them down to the cellar. He had never used the washing machine, unlike the dishwasher, but he found a manual on the shelf with the detergents and followed the instructions. One load comprised two sets of bedding; he would need to run four or five loads.

He walked to the lake and sat on the bench. With the sounds of his grandchildren playing and swimming it was a place like the table in the library or the café, or the sofa in the living room—he was with the others and yet on his own. Without the sounds he was just lonely. He wanted to go over what he should do, but nothing occurred to him. Then he wanted to think over one of the philosophical problems he'd taken with him into retirement, and not only did nothing occur to him with regard to one of the problems, no problem occurred to him, either. Situations from the last week came to his mind: David and Meike in the boat, Matthias and Ferdinand building the island, Ariane with the book on her knees, he and Ariane with the painter, cooking with the children, trimming the hedge, the tea and lemonade for his wife, their growing intimacy, the morning when they made love. He felt a breath of desire, just a breath, because he hadn't yet fully grasped that they had all left. He knew it was so, he had heard it with his own ears and seen it with his own eyes, but he hadn't yet fully grasped it.

When the pain made its entrance, he was almost happy. The way you are almost happy when you find yourself alone in a strange place and then you meet someone you don't like, but with whom you share a past at school or university or in a business or an office. The encounter distracts you from the loneliness. And the pain also made him remember why he was here: not to be wrapped up in his family but to take leave of it. Now leave-taking had simply happened a little earlier and a little differently.

That's the way it was. Or was it? He stood, intending to hang the first load of laundry out to dry and put the next load in. Before he even reached the house he knew that this morning's leave-taking hadn't just arrived a little early and a little differently. It had nothing in common with the leave-taking that he had envisioned. The leave-taking that has happened is over. The leave-taking that you envision still contains the possibility that it can be delayed or prevented, or that a miracle can intervene. He didn't believe in miracles. But he realized that he had imagined something. He had imagined that the pain would get steadily worse, steadily less bearable, until it became unbearable and the decision to take his leave would make itself. Instead of which the medicine had got stronger along with the pain. The decision to drink the cocktail and depart was not going to make itself. He had to decide, and because there had still been time, he hadn't allowed himself to know how hard it was. If he broke his arm or his leg—would that be when the time came?

He had sometimes seen his wife hanging out washing. She wiped off the clothesline that was stretched across the garden, carried the laundry basket up out of the cellar, shook out the pieces of laundry, and attached them firmly with clothespins that she took out of a sack she had tied around her waist like an apron. That was what he did too. Bending over to pick up each piece, shaking it out, taking the pins out of the sack, stretching up to the line, and attaching the pieces firmly to it—with every movement he saw his wife in front of him, no, he felt her make each movement. He was seized by a physical sympathy with his wife's body, which had withstood the demands of a job and the house and the children, the pains of childbirth and a miscarriage, susceptibility to bladder infections and the assaults of migraines; he felt it so strongly that he began to weep, and wanted to stop but could not. He sat down on the steps of the veranda and watched through his tears as the wind blew through the laundry, letting it sink, and then lifting it again.

Nothing would remain of the last summer he had so carefully constructed. Once again he had had all the components at hand, but happiness had not resulted. This was different from the times before; he had been truly happy for a while. But the happiness hadn't wished to remain.

16

That same day he began to listen. In the garden or by the lake he listened to see whether what he'd just heard was the sound of his wife's car. He was upstairs on the second floor, heard a sound on the first floor, and listened for footsteps. He was on the first floor, heard a sound on the second floor, and listened for voices.

In the next days he was sometimes convinced that he'd heard his wife drive in or come up the stairs or Matthias come running or Ariane calling. He would step outside the door or to the stairs or turn around, and no one was there. One day he kept walking from the house to the lake and back again, because he was convinced that his wife was going to come in a boat, sit on the bench, and wait for him to come and join her. When he was down at the bench, he found the idea absurd. But when he was back in the house, it wasn't long before he thought he heard the engine throttle as the boat docked.

As the emptiness of the house and garden grew in his ears, he let himself go. The morning ritual of showering, shaving, and putting on his clothes was more than his strength could manage. When he drove to buy groceries, he put on his pants over his pajamas and pulled on a jacket and ignored other people's glances. In the afternoons he began to drink, and by evening he was either drunk or, if the alcohol and the pills took effect together, almost unconscious. Only then was he free of the pain. At all other times some part of his body, often his entire body, hurt.

One evening he tripped on the cellar stairs, but was too drunk to get up and climb them. He sat on a step and leaned against the wall and went to sleep. He woke in the night and realized that his right hand was swollen and hurt. It was not the familiar pain but a new, fresh pain that stabbed from the wrist to the fingers every time he moved his hand. It told him the hand was broken. It also told him that the time had come.

But he didn't fetch the bottle. Instead he went into the kitchen and made coffee. He filled a towel with ice cubes, sat down at the table, cooled the hand, and drank his coffee. He wouldn't be able to drive by himself. He'd have to order a taxi. He was embarrassed by the way he looked and smelled and forced himself painfully into the shower and fresh underclothes and a suit. He called the taxi company, roused the old boss from bed whom he'd known for years, and who said he'd come himself, then sat down on the terrace to wait. The night air was warm.

After that, things went of their own accord. The taxi took him to the hospital, the doctor gave him an injection and sent him for an X-ray, the nurse in the X-ray department took the pictures and sent him to the waiting room. He was the only patient, and sat in the white neon light on a white plastic chair looking out onto the empty parking lot. He waited and wrote a letter in his mind to his wife.

It was an hour before he was called. There was a second doctor standing with the first, who took over the conversation and explained the number and composition of bones in the hand, which two were broken, that no operation or splinting was required, that a firm bandage would be sufficient, and everything was going to heal just fine. He applied the bandage and instructed him to come back in three days. Reception would call a taxi for him.

The old boss who'd driven him to the hospital also drove him home. They talked about their children. The sky was growing light and the birds were making the same racket as on the morning when he'd made the pancakes. How long ago was that? Three weeks?

17

He went into his study and sat down at his typewriter. On it he had written letters, essays, and books until he got a secretary to whom he could dictate. He should have taught himself to use the computer in his retirement, but he'd preferred to ask his former secretary or to stop writing.

Using the typewriter was no longer a habit, and he was particularly clumsy without the use of his right hand. He had to use his forefinger to find one letter after the other.

I can't cope without you. Not because of the laundry; I wash and dry and fold it. Not because of meals; I buy things and prepare them. I clean the house and water the garden.

I can't cope without you, because without you everything is nothing. In everything I've done in my life, I've drawn on the fact that I had you. If I hadn't had you, I would never have achieved anything. Since I've no longer had you, I've been steadily disintegrating until I came apart completely. Luckily I had an accident which has brought me to my senses.

I'm sorry I didn't tell you everything about the state I was in, and that I planned to end things by myself, and that I wanted to decide on my own when I couldn't go on any longer.

You know the box I inherited from Father. I'm going to lock the bottle in the box and put the box in the refrigerator.

You'll find the key in this letter; that way I won't be able to make my decision without you. When things can't go on, we'll decide together that they can't go on. I love you.

He locked the bottle in the box, put the box in the refrigerator, put the key and the letter in the envelope, and addressed it to their apartment in the city. He waited for the mailman and gave him the letter to take with him.

The mailman had barely left when he was overtaken by doubt. His life, his death, in her hands? What if she didn't get the letter, or didn't open it, or didn't like it? He would have liked to read over what he had written, but he hadn't made a copy. At least there was an almost complete draft that he'd thrown away because it was full of mistakes. He would find it in the wastepaper basket.

When he was standing in front of his desk he saw a key in the open drawer. He took it out. He'd forgotten there was a second key to the box. He laughed and tucked it away.

He lay down on the sofa in the study and slept the sleep that had eluded him the night before. When the pain in his head woke him two hours later, he walked to the lake and sat on the bench. If she hadn't gone off somewhere, she would get the letter tomorrow. If she were in fact away, it could take days.

He stood up, took the key out of his pocket, and threw it as far as he could with his left hand. The key flashed in the sunlight, then flashed again as it hit the water. A few tiny waves made a circle around the spot. Then the lake was calm again.

Johann Sebastian Bach on Ruegen

1

At the end of the film he wanted to cry. Not that the film had a happy ending—it didn't end with the promise of a happy future, only a vague hope. The couple who were meant for each other missed each other, but perhaps they would meet again. The woman had lost her business, but was going to risk a new start.

She'd lost her business because her sister had done her out of her money. She could risk a new start because her father, a grumpy old man who sometimes took care of her son after a fashion and mostly was full of idiotic ideas, out of nowhere sold his house to give her the delivery van she needed. After that father and daughter stood in the street looking at the van, she with her head on his shoulder and he with his arm around her. Her business was the cleaning of crime scenes, and at the end the father was setting to work with the daughter in blue coveralls, a white face mask, and the kind of intimacy that makes words superfluous.

Happy endings in films more and more often made him want to cry. His chest would tighten, his eyes go damp, and he'd have to clear his throat before he could speak. But the tears didn't come, even though he would have liked to cry, not just at happy endings in the movie theater but also when he was overcome with sadness about the end of his marriage or the death of his friend or simply the loss of his life's hopes and dreams. As a child he had cried himself to sleep—but he couldn't anymore.

The last time he'd been able to cry properly was many years ago. He was having one of those political arguments with his father that were a frequent occurrence in those days between the generations and in which the parents saw everything threatened that they had lived for, and the children everything denied that they wanted to do differently and better. He understood and respected his father's pain over the loss of a world that was familiar and loved; all he also wanted was for his father to understand and respect his own wish for a new world. But his father accused him of being thoughtless and inexperienced, presumptuous, lacking all respect and responsibility, until he wanted to cry. But he didn't want to give his father that triumph. He swallowed his tears and couldn't speak, but stood up to him.

Would his father have sold his house and given him a delivery van if he'd needed it? Would his father have put on blue coveralls and a white face mask and helped him clean crime scenes? He didn't know. For him and his father it wouldn't have been about delivery vans and coveralls and face masks. Would his father have supported him if he'd lost his job because of his political involvements? Helped him to start again in another profession or another country? Or would he have felt it served him right and he didn't deserve any help?

Even if his father had helped him—it would never have happened in the atmosphere of silent intimacy that existed between father and daughter in the movie. It was a miniature happy ending within the large vague ending of the film. It was a tiny miracle. So tears were allowed.

2

He had intended to take a taxi home and get back to work on the article the newspaper wanted to publish at the beginning of next week. But when he came out of the movie theater and felt the soft night air of summer, he decided to walk. Across the square, past the museum, along the river—he was astonished at how lively the streets were. Groups of tourists came toward him, and parents and kids were often out together. He was particularly moved by a group of Italians. Grandfather and grandmother, father and mother, sons and daughters plus their boyfriends and girlfriends came toward him, arms linked, walking lightly, singing quietly, giving him friendly, inquiring, inviting looks, and had passed him before he could even begin to imagine what the inquiry and the invitation might represent and how he might respond. Am I, he wondered, turning sentimental when I see parents and children happy together?

He asked himself the same question again later while he was having a glass of wine in his local Italian restaurant. A father and son were having a lively, friendly conversation two tables over. Then his mood changed; he turned envious, irritable, and bitter. He couldn't remember a single similar conversation with his father. Any time they were talking animatedly, it was an argument over politics or the law or society. The only time they talked in a friendly way was when they were exchanging trivialities.

The next morning his mood changed again. It was Sunday, he had breakfast out on the balcony, the sun shone, thrushes were singing, and the church bells were ringing. He didn't want to be bitter. He also didn't want there to be nothing except tired or bad memories when his father died. When his parents were back from church, he called them. His mother picked up, as she always did, and as always, after the exchange of questions about archives, health, and the weather, the conversation faltered.

"Do you think I could invite Father on a little trip?"

It took some time for her to reply. He knew that there was nothing she wanted more than better relations between her children and her husband. Was she hesitating because she couldn't grasp the pleasure she felt at his question? Or because she was afraid the situation between him and his father was already far gone? Finally she asked, "What sort of a little trip are you thinking of?"

"What Father and I both like is the sea and Bach's music." He laughed. "Can you think of anything else we both like? I can't. In September there's a little Bach festival on Ruegen, and I'm thinking of two or three days with a few concerts and some walks on the beach."

"Without me."

"Yes, without you."

Again there was a pause before his mother answered. As if giving herself a shake, she finally said, "What a lovely idea! Can you write your father a letter? I'm afraid he'll feel pressured on the phone and react negatively. And then he'll soon regret it. But why have to sort things out after the fact when a letter will work better to begin with?"

3

On a Thursday in September he picked up his father in the little town where his parents lived and where he'd grown up. The hotel rooms and concert tickets were booked. He had decided against the larger places with their fine turn-of-the-century houses; his father liked things simple, so they were going to stay in a plain hotel in a little village where the beaches ran on for miles. They would hear the French Suites on Friday afternoon, two Brandenburg Concertos and the Italian Concerto on Saturday evening, and motets on Sunday afternoon. He had printed out the concert programs and gave them to his father when they were on the Autobahn. He had also worked out what he wanted to ask his father along the way: about his childhood and youth and his studies and the beginning of his career. It should all go without any arguments.

"Lovely," said his father when he'd read the programs, and then was silent. He sat upright, legs crossed, arms on the arm-rests, and hands hanging down. That was the way he sat in his armchair at home and that was also how he'd seen him when he paid a visit to him in court before he finished high school and witnessed him during a trial. He seemed relaxed, and the angle of his head and the hint of a smile indicated that he was focused and listening carefully. At the same time it was a pos-ture that spoke of distance; it was the relaxed body language of someone who doesn't relate to people or situations, who's hid-ing behind his smile and listening with great skepticism. Since to his own horror he'd caught himself on several occasions sit-ting the same way as his father, he knew what it signified.

He asked him about his earliest memory and learned about the sailor suit his father had been given for Christmas when he was three. He asked about what he'd liked and hated in school, and his father became more talkative and told him about doing drill at gym, and patriotic history lessons and the difficulty he had writing essays until he started imitating articles he read in a book he found in his father's cupboard. He told him about dancing classes and gatherings of the twelfth graders where people drank the way they drank in student clubs and after-ward the ones who felt particularly grown-up went to broth-els. No, he'd never gone along, and he'd never kept pace with their drinking, either, except halfheartedly. He'd refused to join any fraternity when he was a student although his father pushed him to. He'd wanted to study and encounter the riches of the mind at university, after the pittance there had been in high school. He talked about professors he'd heard, events he'd attended, and then he got tired.

"You can put the seat back and sleep."

He did so. "I'm just going to rest." But it wasn't long before he was asleep, snoring and occasionally smacking his lips.

His father asleep—he realized he'd never seen this before. He couldn't remember as a child ever having rolled around in bed with his parents, or gone to sleep or woken up with them. They had taken their holidays without the children; he and his brothers and sister had been sent to their grandparents or aunts and uncles. He liked this; holidays were freedom not just from school but from his parents too. He looked over at his father, saw the stubble on his chin and cheeks, the hairs growing out of his nose and his ears, the spittle in the corner of his mouth, and the burst blood vessels around his nose. He also smelled his father's smell, a little stale and a little sour. He was glad that aside from the ritual hello and goodbye kisses, which mostly he could avoid, there was no intimacy between his parents and him either now or in earlier days. Then he wondered if he'd feel more affectionate toward his father's body if there had been.

He stopped for gas, and his father turned on his side as best he could and kept on sleeping. While he was stuck in traffic, an ambulance cut its way through with flashing blue lights and the siren going, and his father murmured something but didn't wake up. His father's deep sleep annoyed him; it struck him as an expression of the clear conscience with which his father had gone self-righteously through life, judging and condemning him. But then the traffic jam broke up, he drove around Berlin, through Brandenburg, and reached Mecklenburg. The bare landscape fitted his melancholy mood, and the onset of dusk was suitably mild.

"How still the world and in the shroud of twilight how

intimate and fair." His father was awake and quoting Matthias Claudius. He smiled at him and his father smiled back. "I dreamed about your sister, when she was small. She climbed up a tree, higher and higher, and then flew into my arms, as light as a feather."

His sister was the child of his father's first wife, who had died in childbirth, and was known in the family as heavenly mother, as opposed to his second wife, who was present here as earthly mother. His second wife was the mother of his two sons and had also become mother to his sister; the children had always regarded themselves as fully related, never as half brothers and sister. But he had sometimes wondered if his father's particular love for his sister was an extension of his love of his first wife. The twilight, his smile, the telling of his dream as an acknowledgment of longing and a sign of trust—he thought he could ask his father a question. "What was your first wife like?"

His father didn't reply. They drove from twilight into darkness, and his face became invisible and unreadable. He cleared his throat but said nothing. When his son was about to give up hope of a response, the father said, "Oh, not so different from Mama."

4

The next morning he woke up early. Lying in bed he wondered if his father had evaded him or had nothing more he could say about his first wife than he had said. Had he made the two women into a single person in his thoughts and feelings, because he couldn't bear the tension of remembering and mourning and forgetting?

These were not questions he could ask his father over breakfast. They sat on the terrace with a view out over the sea. His father passed on greetings from Mama, to whom he'd just spoken on the phone, cut the top off his egg, put ham on one half of his roll and cheese on the other, and ate with silent concentration. When he'd finished, he read the paper.

What did he and his mother have to talk about on the phone? Did they just tell each other how they'd slept and what the weather was like here and back there? Why did he call her Mama, when none of the children did? Was he interested by the newspaper or just hiding behind it? Did he feel trapped by this journey with his son?

"I expect you're pleased that the government . . ."

It sounded as if his father wanted to launch into one of their customary political arguments. He didn't let him finish. "I haven't read the paper for days. Not till next week. Shall we take a walk on the beach?" His father insisted on reading the rest of the paper, but stopped trying to draw him into an argument. Finally he folded the paper and laid it on the table. "Shall we?"

They walked along the shore, his father in a suit and tie and black shoes, he in shirt and jeans, his sneakers tied by the laces and hanging over his shoulder. "You were talking about your student days on the way here—what came next? Why didn't you have to fight in the war? What exactly was the reason you lost your position as a judge? Did you like being a lawyer?"

"Four questions at once! Back then I already had the arrhythmia I still have now; that's what saved me from the war. I lost my position as a judge because I gave the Confessional Church legal advice. That angered both the president of the State Court and the Gestapo. So I became a lawyer and as such continued to advise the church. My partners in the law firm didn't hinder me; I had almost no involvement in regular legal work like contracts and forming companies and arranging mortgages and drawing up wills, and I almost never appeared in court."

"I read the essay you wrote in 1945 in the *Tageblatt*. No hatred for the Nazis, no settling of accounts, no retaliation, pull together to cope with need, pull together to rebuild shattered towns and villages, solidarity with the refugees—why so forgiving? The Nazis did worse things, I know, but they did also destroy your position."

They made slow progress in the sand. His father made no move to take off his shoes and socks and roll up his trousers, but walked awkwardly, step by step. He didn't care that they would never get to the end of the long, shining beach this way and reach Cape Arkona—but he was sure his father did, because he always had goals and made plans, and had asked questions about the Cape at breakfast. In three hours they had to be back at the hotel.

Once again he was ready to give up hope of any answer when his father said, "You can't imagine what it's like when life goes off the rails. The only thing that matters then is to reestablish order."

"The president of the State Court . . ."

". . . greeted me amicably in the fall of 1945 as if I'd just returned from an extended holiday. He wasn't a bad judge or a bad president. He'd gone off the rails like everyone, and like everyone he was glad it was over."

He saw the beads of sweat on his father's forehead and cheeks. "Would you go off the rails if you took off your jacket and tie and went barefoot?"

"No." He laughed. "Maybe I'll try that tomorrow. Today I'd like to sit down by the sea and look at the waves. How about right here?" He didn't say whether he couldn't go on or whether he didn't want to. He hitched up his trouser legs so they wouldn't crease at the knees, sat down cross-legged on the sand, looked out to sea, and said nothing more.

He sat down beside his father. Once he'd rid himself of the feeling that they somehow had to talk to each other, he began to enjoy the view out over the sea, the white clouds, the interplay of sun and shade, the salty air, and the light breeze.

"How come you read my essay from 1945?" It was the first question his father had asked him since they'd set out, and he couldn't detect whether it was mistrustful or merely curious.

"I did a favor for a colleague at the *Tageblatt* and he sent me a copy of your piece. I'm guessing he checked in the archives to see if there was anything that might interest me."

His father nodded.

"Were you afraid when you were advising the Confessional Church?"

His father uncrossed his legs, stretched them in front of him, and propped himself on his elbows. It looked uncomfortable and clearly was, because after a time he sat up again and went back to sitting cross-legged. "For a long time I intended to write something about fear. But when I retired and had the time, I didn't do it."

5

The concert began at five. When they parked at four thirty in front of the castle in which the concert was taking place in the great hall, most of the parking spots were empty. He suggested they use the time before the concert began to take a walk in the castle gardens. But his father was insistent, so they sat down in the front row of the empty hall and waited.

"It's the first time Ruegen has organized a Bach festival."

"People need time to get used to everything. At first they had to get used to Bach's music too. You know it was Mendelssohn who discovered him and reintroduced him in the nineteenth century?" His father talked about Bach and Mendelssohn, about the evolution of the Suite as an assemblage of dances in the sixteenth century, about the appearance of the name Partita alongside Suite in the seventeenth century, about Bach's suites and partitas as the works in which he emphasized lightness, about the early drafts of some of the suites in the *Little Notebook for Anna Magdalena Bach,* about the origin of the French Suites, the English Suites, and the Partitas between 1720 and 1730, about the three French Suites in minor keys and the three in major keys, and their various movements. He talked animatedly, enjoying his own knowledge and his son's attentiveness, and stressed how much he looked forward to the concert.

A young pianist whom neither father nor son had ever heard of played with cold precision, as if the tones were numbers and as if the suites were calculations. His bow to the small audience at the end of his performance was just as cold.

"Would he have played with more heart in front of a larger audience?"

"No, he thinks that's how Bach is to be played. He thinks the way we like hearing Bach is sentimental. But isn't it splendid? No interpretation can harm Bach, not even this one. Not even being used as a ringtone—I'm sitting in the tram, I hear a cell phone, and it's still Bach and it's still good." The father was talking warmly. On their way to the hotel he compared Richter's and Schiff's and Fellner's and Gould's and Jarrett's interpretations of the French Suites and the son was as impressed by his father's knowledge as he was alienated by the sheer flow of words that kept pouring on and on—uninterruptedly, obliviously, impervious to any question or comment. It was like his father was talking to himself.

Over dinner it just went on. The father turned from the interpretation of the French Suites to that of the masses, oratorios, and passions. When the son finally returned from a long visit to the toilet, the flood of words had ceased, but the father's animation, his joy and warmth, had vanished along with it. The son ordered a second bottle of red wine and was prepared to get a comment from the father about extravagance and gluttony. But the father accepted another glass gladly.

"Where do you get your love for Bach?"

"What a question!"

The son didn't give up. "There are reasons why one person loves Mozart and another loves Beethoven and the third one loves Brahms. What interests me is why you love Bach."

Once again the father sat upright, one leg crossed over the other, arms on the chair arms and the hands dangling down, head bent, and the hint of a smile. He was staring into the blue. The son observed the father's face, the high forehead under a still-full head of gray hair, the deep grooves above the nose and running from the nose to the corners of the mouth, the pronounced cheekbones and flabby cheeks, the thin lips, the tired mouth and strong chin. It was a good face, the son could see that, but he didn't see what lay behind it, which worries had carved the furrows in the forehead, which ones had made the mouth weary, why the gaze was empty.

"Bach made me . . ." He shook his head and started again. "Your grandmother was a sparkling, capricious woman, and your grandfather a conscientious bureaucrat, not devoid of . . ."

Again he stopped. The son had visited the grandmother in a home with his father several times; she sat in a wheelchair, didn't speak, and from a conversation between father and doctor he gleaned an impression that she was depressed in her old age. He hadn't ever consciously known his grandfather. Why couldn't the father talk about his parents? "Bach reconciles opposites. The light and the dark, the strong and the weak, the past . . ." He shrugged his shoulders. "Perhaps it was just that with Bach I learned to play the piano. For two years I was allowed to play nothing but études, and after that the *Little Notebook* was a gift from heaven."

"You played the piano? Why don't you play anymore? When did you stop?"

"I wanted to take lessons again when I retired, but it didn't happen." He stood up. "Shall we take a walk along the beach after breakfast tomorrow? I think Mama packed me a suitable pair of pants." He put his hand on his son's shoulder for a moment. "Good night, my boy."

6

When he thought back later about the trip with his father, the Saturday was all blue sky and blue sea, sand and cliffs, beach and pine woods, fields and music.

They set off after breakfast, he in jeans and a shirt again with his sneakers over his shoulder; his father in pale linen trousers, a sweater around his hips, and sandals in his hand. When the sand came to an end, they put on their shoes. They made good progress and after several hours they reached the Cape. They didn't talk. When he asked his father if he'd really like to keep going or would rather turn back, his father only shook his head.

At the Cape they rested, again without talking, called a taxi to take them home, sat silently in it, and looked out at the landscape. In the hotel they relaxed until it was time to go to the concert in town. The school hall was full, and father and son were united wordlessly in their pleasure at the energy that the players brought to the music. "I'm glad they're playing the Fourth Brandenburg with flutes, not recorders," was his father's only comment.

In the hotel they ate a light, late supper, hoped for good weather the next day, planned an expedition to the chalk cliffs after breakfast, and wished each other a good night.

He took the half-full bottle of wine to his room with him and sat out on the balcony. His shared time with his father had been as wordless as the father's and daughter's work together at the end of the movie. But it had felt more like a silent truce than wordless intimacy; his father didn't want to be pressured again, he wanted to be left in peace, and he had left him in peace. Why did his questions pressure his father? Because he didn't want to turn his insides out, particularly in front of his son? Because his insides, where the doors and windows had never been opened, were all shriveled and dead, and he didn't know what his son wanted of him? Because he'd grown up before psychoanalysis and psychotherapy had made revelations a daily occurrence and he had no language to communicate his inner feelings? Because whatever he'd done and whatever happened to him, from his two marriages to his professional obligations before and after 1945, he saw in it such a continuity that it was in fact the same and there was nothing to say about it?

He would talk to his father again tomorrow. Wordless intimacy had been too much to hope for. Nor could he hope for loquacious intimacy. But he wanted to reach him. After his death he wanted to have more of him than a photograph on the desk and memories he could have done without.

He recalled his father's awkward, impatient attempts to teach him to swim, the boring, joyless walks he took with him and his brother after church twice a year on Sunday, the inquisitions about his achievements at school and university, the tortuous political arguments, his father's anger when he got divorced, the first divorce in the family. He did not find a single cheering event he could remember.

There was nothing between him and his father, nothing. And the nothing made him so sad that his chest felt tight and his eyes were damp. But the tears didn't come.

7

Only when they were in sight of the chalk cliffs did his father tell him he'd already been on Ruegen before. The first time on his honeymoon with his first wife, the second time on his honeymoon with his second. The goal on both honeymoons had been to reach Hiddensee, and the detour to the chalk cliffs both times had been too long. He was happy he was seeing them at last.

At lunch he asked, "Which motets are they singing this afternoon?"

The son got up and fetched the program: "Fear thou not; for I am with thee" (Isaiah 41:10); "the Spirit also helpeth our infirmities" (Romans 8:26); "Jesu My Joy," "Sing Unto the Lord a New Song."

"Do you know the texts?"

"The texts of the motets? Do you?"

"Yes."

"All the motets? And the cantatas?"

"There are hundreds of cantatas and very few motets. I sang

them in choir when I was a student. 'Fear thou not, for I am with thee: be not dismayed; for I am thy God: I will strengthen thee; yea, I will help thee; yea, I will uphold thee with the right hand of my righteousness.' A fine text for a law student."

"I know you go to church every Sunday. Out of habit or because you really believe?" He knew he was asking a difficult question. His father had been deeply saddened to realize that his three children rejected church from an early age, but he allowed this to be known only by the troubled expression on his face as he stood up from the breakfast table on Sunday mornings and set off for church without them. He had never spoken to them about religion.

His father leaned back. "Faith is a habit."

"It becomes that, but it doesn't begin as a habit. How did you start to become a believer?" That was an even more difficult question. His mother had once mentioned that his father, who had grown up without religion, had experienced a conversion as a student. But how the conversion had occurred was something she didn't say, and his father had also never even spoken about it as a fact.

He leaned even further back and his hands gripped the ends of the chair arms. "I . . . I always hoped . . ." He looked into the blue. Then he slowly shook his head. "You have to experience it yourself. If you don't have it yourself . . ."

"Talk to me. Mother once mentioned that you underwent a conversion when you were a student. It must have been the most important thing that ever happened to you—how can you not tell your own children about it? Don't you want us to know you? And know what's important to you, and why? Don't you notice what a distance there is between us? Do you think it was just their jobs that sent your daughter to San Francisco and your elder son to Geneva? How much longer do you want to wait before you talk to me?" He was getting more and more agitated. "Don't you realize that children want more from their father than measured behavior and silent distance and the occasional argument about politics that's forgotten by morning? You're eighty-two and one day you'll be dead, and the only thing I'll have of you is the desk I've liked since I was a child and which my brother and sister have always said I could have. And one day I'll catch myself sitting exactly the way you're sitting now, because I'll want as little to do with the person sitting opposite me as you want with me now." He wished he could just get up and leave.

A scene from his childhood flashed into his mind. He must have been ten when he brought home a little black cat that the brother of a playmate was supposed to drown in the river along with the rest of the litter. He looked after the cat, taught it to keep itself clean, fed it, played with it, and loved it; his father, who didn't like the animal, tolerated it. But when the family were having supper one evening and the cat jumped onto the grand piano, his father stood up and swiped it away with an urgent gesture, as if banishing dust. He felt as if his father had wiped him away too, and was so upset and undone that he jumped up, seized the cat, and left the apartment. But where could he go? After three hours out in the cold, he came back home, his father opened the door to him silently, and having to face him was as bad as being wiped away by him. After a few weeks the cat gave him asthma and was given away.

His father looked at him. "I think you know me. It wasn't like being the young Martin Luther and lightning striking the tree right next to him. You mustn't think I've been holding back something dramatic from you." Then he looked at his watch. "I should have a little rest. When do we have to leave?"

8

He knew he shared his father's love for Bach, but had only ever been interested in secular music. His Bach was the Bach of the Goldberg Variations, the Suites and Partitas, the Musical Offering, and the concertos. As a child he had gone with his parents to the St. Matthew Passion and the Christmas Oratorio and had been bored, which had led him to the belief that Bach's religious music was not for him. If they hadn't fit into the program for his trip with his father, he would never have thought of listening to the motets.

But when he was sitting in the church listening to the music, it took hold of him. He didn't understand the texts, and because he didn't want to distract himself from the music by reading the words, he didn't follow along in the program, either. He wanted to savor the sweetness of the music. Sweetness was something he had never associated with Bach, nor in his view should it be. But what he was experiencing was sweetness, sometimes painful, sometimes soulful, profoundly at peace in the chorales. He remembered his father's answer to his question about why he loved Bach.

During the interval they stepped outside the church and watched the bustle of a summer Sunday afternoon. Tourists wound their way across the square or sat at tables outside cafés and restaurants, children ran around the fountain, smells of frying sausages and a general babble of voices filled the air. The world inside the church and the world outside it couldn't have been more of a contrast. But this didn't irritate him. He made his peace with it too.

Again they didn't talk, not during the interval, and not on the drive back to the hotel. Over dinner his father became expansive, and lectured about Bach's motets, their role in weddings and funerals, their performance originally with an orchestra, but since the nineteenth century unaccompanied, and their place in the repertoire of the Thomas Church choir. After dinner his father suggested a walk along the beach, and they went out into the dusk and returned in full darkness.

"No," he said, "I don't know who you are."

His father laughed softly. "Or you don't like it." Back at the hotel he asked, "When do we leave tomorrow?"

"I have to be home by evening, and would like to leave here early. Can we have breakfast at seven thirty?"

"Yes. Sleep well."

Again he went to sit on the balcony outside his room. That was it. He could ask his father things about his studies and his work on the way back. But why? He wasn't going to learn what he wanted to learn.

He'd lost the desire to question his father. After all their mutual silences, the prospect of an equally silent journey home didn't bother him anymore.

9

They didn't drive in total silence. There were the signs on the Autobahn announcing this attraction or that, which roused his father to a recollection or a lesson. Or the traffic news came on the radio to report jams or slow-moving traffic, even a horse loose on the highway, and his father noted that these weren't affecting them. Or his father noticed that he slowed down ahead of a gas station, asked if he needed to gas up, and he explained he was deciding whether to do that here or at the next one. Or he asked his father if he'd like to stop for a coffee, or lunch, or whether he'd like to put the seat back and sleep.

He was attentive, polite, and obliging to his father, behaving as he would also have behaved if he'd felt a connection to him. But he didn't feel any connection; he was cold and far away. He thought about what was awaiting him at the newspaper the next day, the column, the series with portraits, and the big article about alimony reform that he was due to deliver next week. Was his father using all his recollections and lectures and statements and questions to try to start a conversation? He no longer cared, and remained monosyllabic.

When there was still an hour to go before he could deposit his father, they drove into a storm. He turned up the wipers faster and faster, but finally they couldn't contend with the rain. He drove onto the verge under a bridge and stopped. The drumming of the rain on the car roof stopped from one moment to the next. Other cars' tires hissed on the wet roadway, but otherwise it was still.

"I could . . ." He had a CD player in the car, but usually no CDs. When he was driving alone he worked, making calls and dictating. If he was tired and needed to stay awake, he turned on the radio. But after yesterday's concert he'd bought one of the choir's recordings that had Bach motets. He put it in.

Again he was seized by the sweetness of the music. Now he also heard fragments of the texts. "Thou art mine, because I hold Thee, and let Thee not out of my heart"—he would not have said it in those words, but that was what he had felt when he loved his wife and knew that she loved him. "For all flesh *is* as grass, and all the glory of man as the flower of grass. The grass withereth, and the flower thereof falleth away. . . ."— how well he knew that feeling, how often it occurred in his life as he raced from task to task and appointment to appointment. "Beneath thy shelter I am safe from the storms of mine enemies"—that is how he felt, sheltered by the bridge and free from the raging not just of this storm but all the storms to come.

Wanting to make some comment about the texts, he looked over at his father. He was sitting the way he always sat, legs crossed, arms on the armrests, hands dangling down. And tears were streaming down his face.

At first he couldn't take his eyes off his weeping father. Then he felt he was being intrusive, and turned away to look out at the rain. Was his father also looking out at the rain, at the rain and the road and the cars that were driving through a puddle beyond the bridge, covered in flying drops and sending up great sprays of water? Or was everything invisible to his father behind his veil of tears?

Not just the rain and the road, but everything that didn't bow to his need for continuity and balance? Had his children, with their changes, their false starts, and their rebelliousness, made him so sad that he didn't want to see them? "A pity they'll grow up," he'd said to his daughter when he met her two-year-old twins at his wife's seventieth-birthday party.

They stayed parked under the bridge till the storm was over and the music had come to an end. Then his father wiped a handkerchief over his face and folded it neatly. He smiled at his son. "I think we can drive."

The Journey to the South

1

The day she stopped loving her children was no different from other days. When she asked herself the next morning what had triggered the loss of love, she could find no answer. Had the pains in her back been particularly tormenting? Had her failure at some domestic task been particularly humiliating? Had an argument with the staff been particularly upsetting? It must have been some such small thing. No big thing happened in her life anymore.

But whatever the cause, the loss was there. She had picked up the phone to call her daughter and discuss her birthday, the guests, the place, the food, and then she had hung up again. She didn't want to talk to her daughter. Nor did she want to talk to any other of her children. She didn't want to see her children, not on her birthday and not before and not after. Then she sat by the phone and waited for the desire to make calls to reassert itself. But it didn't. When the phone rang in the evening, she picked up only because otherwise her children would have been worried enough to call the receptionist and send the staff to check on her. She preferred to lie and say she couldn't talk, she had visitors.

She had no reason to find fault with her children. She was lucky with them. Even the other women in the retirement home told her how good her relations with them were. How successful her children were: one son a high judge, the other the director of a museum, one daughter married to a professor, and the other married to a well-known conductor! How carefully they looked after her! They came to visit, didn't allow too much time to pass between visits by one or the other of them, stayed for one or two nights, sometimes collected her to come and spend two or three days with them, and brought their families to visit on birthdays. They helped her with her tax returns, insurance and pension issues, went with her to the doctor and to get glasses and hearing aids. They had their own families, their own professions, and their own lives. But they let their mother share in them.

She went to bed with the feeling of something the matter with her, the way when you have a stomach upset you go to bed with a Rennie tablet or when you're starting a cold you go to bed with an aspirin, so as to wake up the next morning with nothing wrong. She had nothing to take against loss of love, but she made tea, a mixture of chamomile and mint, and was sure that everything would be back in order the next morning. But the next morning, imagining seeing her children or talking to them on the phone was as alien as it had been the evening before.

2

She took the same walk she took every morning: past the school, the post office, the pharmacy, and the greengrocer, through the housing development to the wood, along the slope to the Bierer Hof and back again. The stretch of land always offered a view down onto the plain, which she loved. The plain was flat, and the walk took no more than an hour. The doctor had told her she must walk for at least an hour every day.

The rain of the last few days had stopped during the night, the sky was blue, and the air was fresh. The day was going to turn hot. She heard the woodland noises: the wind in the trees, sparrows and cuckoos, the creak of branches and the rustle of leaves. She kept a lookout for deer and hares; they were numerous around here and totally without fear. She would like to have smelled the wood, still wet from the rain but warmed by the sun, the way it smelled best. But a couple of years ago she had lost her sense of smell. It had simply disappeared one day, like her love for her children. A virus, said the doctor.

Her sense of taste had disappeared along with it. Food had never meant much to her, so being unable to taste things wasn't so bad. What was bad was being unable to smell nature anymore, not just the wood but the fruit trees in blossom, the flowers on the balcony and in the vase, the warm dry dust in the streets when the first raindrops fell on it.

Aside from this she found the loss of her sense of smell humiliating. Being able to smell is part of a functioning life. Like sight and hearing and walking and reading and writing and being able to count. She had always functioned, and all of a sudden she wasn't functioning anymore, not because of some external intervention, but because her physical equipment had failed. With it came the fear that she might be stinking. She remembered her visit to her mother in the old-age home. "They can't smell things anymore," her mother had explained when she made a remark about the old people's smell. Did she stink like that too now? She was scrupulously clean, and used an eau de toilette that her granddaughters liked. "How nice you smell, Grandmother!" But you never know, and if you use too much, you can stink of eau de toilette, too.

Aside from her doctor, no one knew about her loss of the sense of taste and smell. She praised the food when her children took her out, and sniffed the bunches of flowers they brought with them. When she showed them the flowers on the balcony, she said, "Smell them, they're wonderful."

That was how she must deal with the loss of love too. Along with seeing and hearing and smelling and walking and reading and writing and counting you're also supposed to love your children and your grandchildren. Refusing to make a phone call, the way she had yesterday—no, she wouldn't permit herself to do that again. The birthday would be celebrated as usual and visits would go on the way they always had. Another memory surfaced. When she was a little girl, she had asked her mother, who had married a widower with two children and difficult, demanding parents, brothers, and sisters-in-law, whether she loved these relatives of the first wife whom she had to take care of.

Her mother had smiled. "Yes, darling."

"But . . ."

"Love isn't a matter of feeling, it's a matter of will."

She had achieved this over years, even decades, and she could achieve it no longer. With sheer willpower you can make a duty into an inclination and a responsibility into a love. But she no longer had any responsibility for her children and no duty to her grandsons and granddaughters. There was nothing in the situation that she could will into becoming love. But there was no reason to offend the children, who'd turned out so well, and to irritate the other women in the home and embarrass herself.

She had started her walk with elation. The emptiness left by the disappearance of her love for her children had startled her, but had also made her feel light-headed. She was elated the way you are when you have a high fever or after a long fast—it's a state that must be remedied and yet feels good. As she was sitting on the bench outside the Bierer Hof, she felt herself become heavy and tired and knew that she was coming back down to earth again.

Should she have her birthday party here at the Bierer Hof? When she was still married, she and her husband had sometimes driven here to take a walk and have a coffee. The hours thus spent were stolen, his from work, hers from the children, to talk about all the things that there was never time to talk about in their daily routine. Until one day he drove her here and confessed that for the last two years he'd been sleeping with his assistant.

Since then things had been built on, rebuilt, done up. The inn, shabby back then, looked well tended, and the interior would certainly retain nothing of the atmosphere of the little room in which her husband had sat opposite her and squirmed and wanted her sympathy for his heart, which was big enough to love two women. The memory, so hurtful for so long, no longer hurt. Even now, she didn't feel the sympathy her husband had been seeking, but a sad indifference toward this man who had always found the easy way through life while believing he was doing things the hard way and struggling and fighting. She would gladly have spared herself the later years of her marriage. But he insisted on staying with her until their youngest child had finished school. In the last year he even ended the affair with his assistant. Insufficiently rewarded by his wife for these two sacrifices, he began the next affair with his next assistant.

She got up and started back. Life would go on as if nothing had happened. If only she could stop living for other people and finally live her own life! But it wasn't just that she was too old for it. She had no idea what her own life actually was. Finally doing what gave her pleasure? The only pleasure she had ever learned was to satisfy her responsibilities with love and to fulfill her duties. Then of course there was also nature. But she could no longer smell that.

3

On the morning of her birthday she made herself look beautiful. Lilac knitted suit, white blouse with white embroidery and a white bow, lilac shoes. The hairdresser she used to go to came and curled her hair. "If I were an older gentleman, I would pay court to you. And if I were your granddaughter, I'd be so proud I'd show you off to all my friends."

Everyone came. The four children, their spouses, and the thirteen granddaughters and grandsons. On the way to the Bierer Hof the sons and sons-in-law made one group and the daughters and daughters-in-law another; the elder grandsons and granddaughters joined in conversations about school-leaving exams and university while the younger ones were engrossed in talk of pop music and computer games. She walked with each group for a while, first welcomed and then amiably overlooked as conversation switched back to where it had been interrupted. This didn't bother her. But whereas she would have been happy before that her loved ones got along so well together amid all the marriages and individual families, now she wondered what it was they had to talk about. Pop music and computer games? Which university degrees led to rich careers? Should they try Botox? How to find a cheap holiday in the Seychelles?

Aperitifs were served on the terrace, lunch at a long table in the adjoining room. After the soup the eldest son made a speech. Memories of the time when the children were young, celebration of how she had engaged herself in the life of the community after the children had left home, thanks for the love with which she had accompanied both children and grandchildren and accompanied them still—all of it a little dry, but well meant and well delivered. She pictured him leading a meeting or a conference. Her husband, her marriage, her divorce were not mentioned; it made her think of photographs out of the Russian Revolution that Stalin had retouched to eliminate Trotsky. As if he'd never existed.

"Do you think I couldn't bear it if you mentioned your father? That I didn't know you see him and his wife? Or that you celebrated his eightieth birthday with them? You were all there in the picture in the newspaper!"

"You've never once mentioned him since he moved out. So we thought . . ."

"You thought? Why didn't you ask?" One after the other, she gave her children a searching look, and the children looked back at her, puzzled. "Instead of asking, you thought. You thought if I don't mention him, that means I can't bear you to mention him. Did you think I'd crack? Or weep or scream or thrash about? Or forbid you to meet him? Or make you choose: him or me?" She shook her head.

It was her youngest daughter who spoke again. "We were afraid you . . ."

"Afraid? You were afraid of me? I'm so strong that I make you afraid, and so weak that I can't cope if you mention your father? That makes no sense!" She realized she was getting louder and sharper. Now the grandchildren were looking at her crossly too.

Her eldest son jumped in. "Everything in its own time. Each of us had our own history with Father, each of us is glad to be able for once to talk to you in peace about him. But right now we don't want to hold up the waitresses from serving the next course, otherwise their whole program will be thrown off."

"The waitresses' whole program . . ." She saw the pleading look on her youngest daughter's face and said no more. It wasn't difficult to remain silent over the salad, the sauerbraten, and the chocolate mousse. Everyone was talking, and she had to make an effort to hear what her neighbor or the person opposite her was saying. That's what always happened to her when a lot of people were talking; her doctor had a name for it: party deafness, and the prognosis that nothing could be done about it. She had learned to turn to the person opposite her in a friendly way, to smile companionably from time to time, or nod, all while thinking about something else. Mostly her opposite number didn't notice a thing.

Before the coffee, her youngest granddaughter, Charlotte, stood up and tapped a spoon on her glass until everyone was paying attention. Her uncle had made a speech about their mother, now she wanted to make a speech about their grandmother. All of them sitting here, that is, her grandsons and granddaughters, had learned to read from their grandmother. Not words and sentences, they'd been taught that in school, but books. Whenever they were with her on holidays, their grandmother had read to them. She never got to the end of the book before the end of the holidays, but the book was always so exciting that they had to keep reading it all the way to the end themselves. Soon after school began again, Grandmother sent another book by the same author that they also had to read. "It was so wonderful that we persuaded Gran'fa and Anni to do the same. Thank you, Grandmother, for making us readers and giving us the joy we take in books."

Everyone applauded, and Charlotte came around the table with her glass. "Many, many happy returns, Grandmother!" She clinked glasses and gave her a kiss

In the momentary silence, as Charlotte was returning to her seat and before conversation started up again, she asked, "Who's Anni?" She asked although she knew this must be her ex-husband's second wife and that her question would embarrass the others.

"Anna is Father's wife. The children call Grandfather Gran'fa and Anna Anni." Her oldest son spoke calmly and matter-of-factly.

"Father's wife? You don't mean me—do you mean Father's second wife? Or is there already a third?" She knew she was being difficult. She didn't mean to be, she just couldn't stop.

"Yes, Anna is Father's second wife."

"Anni," she pronounced the "i" ironically, "Anni. I suppose I should be thankful you don't call her Granni and make her your second grandmother. Or do you sometimes call her Granni?" When no one answered, she asked again. "Charlotte, how is it, do you sometimes call Anni Granni?"

"No, Grandmother, we only say Anni to Anni."

"And what's she like, Anni whom you don't call Granni?"

Her youngest daughter weighed in. "Please, can we stop with this?"

"We? No. We didn't start this, so we can't stop this. I started it." She stood up. "And I can't stop it. I'm going to lie down for a bit—will you come and pick me up with the car in a couple of hours for tea?"

4

She declined the offers to accompany her and went alone. What had become of her good intentions? At least she had got up and left. She would rather have kept going—could she have managed to get her children to lose control? The judge, to raise his voice and stamp his foot? And the museum director, to throw crockery on the floor or at the wall? And her daughters, to no longer look pleadingly at her but glare with real hate?

When she was picked up by her eldest grandchild, she had

no further desire to provoke or irritate anyone. It was a short journey, and along the way Ferdinand talked about the exam he had to take in a few weeks. She had always found him particularly even-tempered. Now she had to admit that he was particularly boring. She felt tired.

The day after the party she became ill. No sneezing or coughing, no stomach pains or problems with her digestion. She simply had a high fever, against which neither fever-reducing medicines nor antibiotics had any effect. "A virus," said the doctor, shrugging his shoulders. But he called the eldest son, who sent his second daughter to look after her. Emilia was eighteen and waiting to be accepted as a medical student.

Emilia changed the bed linens, rubbed her back and arms with liniment, and put cold compresses on her legs. She brought fresh-squeezed orange juice in the mornings, freshly grated apple at midday, and red wine in the evenings, into which she had beaten the yolk of an egg, plus a steady supply of mint or chamomile tea. She aired out the room several times a day, and insisted several times a day on her taking a few steps through the room and down the corridor. Once a day she ran a bath, lifted her up, and carried her there. Emilia was a strong girl.

It was five days before the fever began to abate. She didn't want to die, but she was so exhausted that she didn't care whether she lived or died, got better or remained ill. Perhaps she even hoped she would remain ill rather than get well again. She liked the feverish haze in which she awoke and out of which she sank into sleep, and that muted everything she saw and heard. Even better, it transformed the rocking of the tree branches outside the window into the dance of a fairy and the song of a blackbird into a sorceress's call. She also loved the intensity with which she felt the heat of the bathwater and the coolness of the liniment on her skin. She even liked the cold shivers that shook her in the first days; it left her demanding warmth and nothing more, no room to think, no room to feel. Ah, and when the warmth did actually reach her!

She became young again. The fever images and dreams were the fever images and dreams of her childhood. With the fairy and the sorceress came shreds of tales she had loved: *Snow-White and Rose-Red, Little Brother and Little Sister, The Many-Furred Creature, Cinderella, Sleeping Beauty.* When the wind blew through the open window, she thought of the king's bride who could command the wind—more than that she couldn't remember. When she was young, she'd been a good skier; she dreamed she was gliding down a white slope, then took off and swayed over woods and valleys and villages. In another dream she had to meet someone, didn't know who or where, only that it was under a full moon, and how the song began that would be the way they recognized each other; when she woke up she felt she'd already dreamed the dream once before, when she was first in love, and she remembered the opening bars of an old hit song. The melody stayed with her all day. Once she dreamed she was at a ball and danced with a man who had only one arm, but who led her so surely and lightly that she didn't have to move her legs; they wanted to dance until morning but before the first gray light of dawn came in the dream, she woke in the real gray light of dawn.

Emilia often sat on the bed and held her hand. How safe and how light her hand felt in the strong hands of the strong young woman! Her thankfulness at being held, nursed, and cared for, at being allowed to be weak, at having to say and do nothing, reduced her to tears. When she cried, she couldn't stop for a long time; her tears of thankfulness became tears of grief over everything in life that had not turned out the way it should have, and tears of loneliness. It felt good to be held by Emilia.

At the same time she felt as lonely as if Emilia weren't there at all.

When she was recovering and the children came to visit, one after the other, it felt the same. The children were there, but she was so lonely, it was as if they weren't. That's the end of love, she thought. Being so alone with someone that you feel they're not present.

Emilia stayed, took her for short little walks and then longer ones, went with her to lunch in the restaurant in the building, and watched television with her in the evenings. She was always around.

"Shouldn't you be studying? Or earning money?"

"I had a job. But your children decided I should dump it and take care of you, and they're paying me the same as I would have been earning otherwise. It wasn't a good job, it doesn't matter at all."

"How long is your job with me?"

Emilia laughed. "Till your children feel you're well again."

"But what if I'm the one who notices first that I'm better?"

"I thought you were pleased that I'm here."

"I don't like it when other people know better than I do how I am and what I need."

Emilia nodded. "I understand that."

5

Could she push Emilia out? The children would take it as proof that she was still unwell, as they had taken her behavior at her birthday as a symptom of her coming illness. Could she maybe bribe Emilia to convince the children that she was cured?

"No," Emilia laughed, "how would I explain to my parents that I suddenly have money? And if I don't tell them and I behave as if I didn't have money, I'll have to get another job again."

That evening she tried again. "Could I not have given you the money as a gift?"

"You've never given any one of us something that you haven't also given all the others. When we were little you never once took one of us on an excursion that you didn't repeat with all the others over the next two or three years."

"That was overdoing things a bit."

"Father always says that without you he would never have become a judge."

"Even so, it was overdoing things a bit. Would you be allowed to make a trip with me? A recuperative trip?"

Emilia looked doubtful. "You mean a health cure?"

"I'd like to get away. The apartment feels like a prison and you like my guard. I'm sorry, but that's how it is, and it would still be that way even if you were a saint." She smiled. "No, it's that way even though you *are* a saint. I would never have made it without you."

"Where do you want to go?"

"South."

"I can't just tell Mother and Father I'm going south with you! We need a destination and a route and stopping places, and they have to know where they can call the police to have them look for us if we don't check in. And how do you want to go? By car? My parents will never allow it. Well, perhaps if I did the driving, but not with you driving. While you were still healthy, they were already talking about calling the police to have you come in and be tested, so that you fail and will no longer be allowed to drive. Now that you're ill . . ."

She listened to her granddaughter in astonishment. How

anxious this strong girl was, and how fixated on her parents. What destination, what route, what stopping places should she give? "Isn't it enough if we say each morning where we'll be that evening? If we say first thing in the morning that we'll be in Zurich by nightfall?"

She didn't want to go to Zurich. She also didn't want to go south. She wanted to go to the city where she'd begun her studies in the late forties. Yes, the city was in the south. But it wasn't "the South." In the spring and fall it got a lot of rain, and in the winter snow. Only in the summer was it seductively beautiful.

At least that was how she saw the city in her mind's eye. She hadn't been there since her student days. Because there had been no opportunity? Because she'd shied away from it? Because she didn't want to lose the magical memory of that last summer, the summer with the student who had only one arm and with whom she danced at the doctors' ball and then again just now in her fever dream? He had worn a dark suit with the left sleeve tucked into the left pocket, he had steered her lightly and confidently with his right arm, and was the best dancer she danced with all evening. Besides which he talked easily, told the story of how he'd lost his arm to a bomb at fifteen as though it were a joke, and spoke of the philosophers he was studying as if they were idiosyncratic friends.

Or had she not been back because she didn't want to be reminded of the pain of parting? He had taken her home after the ball and kissed her at the door and they'd seen each other again the very next day and every day after that until suddenly he went away. It was September, most of the students had left the city, she had stayed because of him and spun her parents, who were expecting her back home, some tale about a practical training course. She accompanied him to the station, and he promised to write, to phone, and to be back soon. But she never heard from him again.

Emilia phoned her parents from out on the balcony. Afterward she reported that her parents had agreed, but expected a call each morning, each noon, and each evening. "I'm responsible, Grandmother, and I hope you won't make it too hard for me."

"You mean I mustn't run away? Or get drunk? Or get tangled up with strange men?"

"You know what I mean, Grandmother."

No, I don't know—but she didn't say that.

6

The next morning Emilia was taking the burden of responsibility more lightly, and looking forward to the trip. She was fascinated that it was to the city where her grandmother had been as old as she herself was now. During the journey she started to ask questions: about the city, about the university, how her courses had been organized, the lives of the students, how their lodgings had been, and what they ate, and what they did for enjoyment, whether what they wanted after the war was to have fun or make money, whether they'd flirted a lot, and what precautions they'd taken.

"Did you meet Gran'fa while you were a student?"

"We met already when we were children; our parents were friends."

"Doesn't sound very exciting. I like exciting. I broke up with Felix because I didn't want to drag any school stuff on to university. The next thing should be the next thing. Felix was okay, but now I want more than okay. I've read that it can work when parents arrange their children's marriages. Not for me. I . . ."

"That's not how it was. Our parents didn't arrange our marriage, they were just friends. We saw each other a couple of times as children, that's all."

"I don't know. Parents give children messages the children aren't even aware of. That the parents aren't necessarily aware of, either. The parents just think their children suit each other because they come from similar families with similar status and similar incomes and it would be great if they got married. They think it every time they see the children together. They make little comments, little insinuations, little encouragements, that attach themselves like little barbs."

And so it went. Emilia had read that girls in the fifties still believed a kiss could make them pregnant. That men filed for divorce the day after the wedding night if they discovered their wives were no longer virgins. That sports were popular with girls, because they could say their hymens had torn during exercise. That young women rinsed their vaginas with vinegar after sex so as not to get pregnant, and stuck themselves with knitting needles to abort. "Am I glad none of it's like that these days. When you got married and you were a virgin, weren't you terrified on your wedding night? Was Gran'fa actually the only man you ever slept with in your life? Don't you feel you missed something?"

While her granddaughter was talking, she looked at her smooth, pretty face, with its bright eyes, its strong chin, its mouth opening and closing busily as it poured out one idiocy after another. She didn't know whether to laugh or tell her off. Was her whole generation like that? Did they all live so exclusively in the present that they only had the most warped concept of the past? She tried to describe the war and the years after the war, the dreams of girls and women back then, the boys and men they met, the relations between the sexes. But her descriptions were faded and dull; she thought so herself.

So she started to talk about herself. When she came to the kiss after the ball, she wished she had left out the story with the one-armed student. But it was already too late.

"What was his name?"

"Adalbert."

That was Emilia's last interruption. She listened raptly and when it came to the farewell on the platform, she took her grandmother's hand. She already sensed that the story was not going to end well.

"What would your parents say if they saw you taking your hand off the wheel?" She slipped her own out of Emilia's grip.

"Did you never hear from him again?"

"He surfaced in Hamburg a few weeks later. But I didn't speak to him. I didn't want to see him."

"Do you know what happened to him?"

"I once saw a book of his in a bookstore. No idea whether he became a journalist or a professor or whatever. I didn't look at the book."

"What was his last name?"

"That's none of your business."

"Don't make such a fuss, Grandmother. I only want to check out what the man has written who loved my grandmother and whom she loved too. I'm sure he loved you as much as you loved him. Do you know the saying: *Now, if not forever, is sometimes better than never*? It's true. The way you tell it, you don't have bitter memories. They're sweet, too. Bittersweet."

She hesitated. "Paulsen."

"Adalbert Paulsen." Emilia was memorizing it.

They had left the Autobahn and were on a little road that followed a winding river. Had they walked along that river back then? On the other bank, where there was no road and no train? Had they stopped to rest at the guesthouse that was reached by a ferry? She wasn't sure if she recognized the guesthouse and then the castle and then the village again. Perhaps it was only the atmosphere created by river and woods and mountains and old buildings that hadn't ever changed. They had had a wonderful walk, with wine and bread and sausage in their backpacks, had swum in the river, and then had lain in the sun.

They would soon be there. It made no sense to go to sleep now. But she dropped off to sleep all the same, and woke up only when Emilia was parking in front of the hotel she'd located that morning on her computer.

7

What had she expected? The houses were no longer gray, they were white and yellow and ocher, even green and blue. The shops were branches of large chains, and where she remembered little hotels and restaurants and bars, there were fast-food joints. Even the bookstore she had loved was part of a chain and was offering nothing but best sellers and magazines. Nonetheless, the river flowed through the city just as it had before, and the little streets were as narrow, and the path up to the castle as steep and the view from the castle as wide as they always had been. She sat down on the terrace with Emilia and looked out on the city and the countryside.

"So? Is it the way you pictured it?"

"Oh, child, just let me sit for a bit and look around. Luckily I didn't picture much."

She was tired, and after they'd eaten dinner on the terrace and found their hotel again, she went to bed even though it was barely eight o'clock. Emilia had asked permission to go wandering a little through the city, and the request had both astonished and moved her. Was Emilia not independent?

Tired though she was, she didn't fall asleep. Outside it was still light, and she could see everything quite clearly: the wardrobe with its three doors, the table against the wall with the mirror over it, to serve as dressing table or desk as required, the two armchairs next to the bookshelf, which had a bottle of water and a glass and a basket of fruit on it, the TV, and the door to the bathroom. The room reminded her of the rooms she had shared with her husband when she was still accompanying him to conferences; it was a room in a decent hotel, indeed even the best hotel, in some small place, and so functional as to be totally without character.

She thought of the room in which she and Adalbert had spent their first night together. There was a bed in it, a chair, a table with an ewer and basin, a mirror above the table, and a hook on the door. It was functional. And yet it had its secrets and magic. Under the severe gaze of the innkeeper's wife, Adalbert and she had taken two single rooms in the country guesthouse. After dinner they went up to their rooms, and although they'd made no arrangement she knew he would come. She had known it that morning already and had packed her finest nightgown. Now she put it on.

With Adalbert here, would this room have character too? Would she have traveled a lot with him too, would she have spent many nights with him in hotels? What would life have become with him? Also a life by the side of a man with many responsibilities, who traveled a great deal and was rarely at home, and had affairs? She couldn't imagine life with Adalbert that way, but she also couldn't imagine it any other way. Thinking about a life with Adalbert made her feel afraid, with a strange sensation of having absolutely nothing under her feet. Because he'd just left her standing?

She had closed the window, and the street noises were muffled: the bright laughter of young women, the loud voices of young men, a car driving slowly through the pedestrians, music from an open window, the tinkling crash as a bottle broke. Had it been dropped by a drunk? She was afraid of drunks, though she was capable of making clear to them immediately in a firm voice that she wouldn't tolerate any trouble. It's strange, she thought, that knowing how to make other people afraid doesn't protect you from feeling afraid yourself.

She got up and went to the bathroom, where she took off her nightgown and looked at herself. The thin arms and legs, the slack breasts and stomach, the thick waist, the wrinkles in her face and neck—no, she didn't like herself. Not the way she looked, not the way she felt, not the way she was living. She put the nightgown on again, lay down in bed, and turned on the television. How easy: all the men and all the women and all the parents and all the children loved one another! Or were they all just playing a game in which each one pretends to the other one so that the other one will allow them their own illusions? Had she simply lost her taste for the game? Or was the investment no longer worth it, because she needed no more illusions in the years that were left to her?

She also needed no more trips. Trips were another illusion, even more short-lived than love. She would go home the next day.

8

But when she knocked on Emilia's door at nine o'clock the following morning, there was no answer, and when she went out onto the terrace where breakfast was being served, Emilia wasn't at any of the tables. She went to Reception and was told that the young lady had gone out half an hour before.

"Did she leave any message?"

No, she hadn't. But after a while the friendly girl from the Reception desk came to the breakfast table to announce that the young lady had telephoned to say she would be back at noon to pick up her grandmother for lunch.

She wasn't happy to be sitting here, trapped. She had wanted to leave at ten, be on the Autobahn by eleven, and home by four. But then she made herself settle down to wait. The sun was shining in the inner courtyard and on the breakfast terrace, and the waiters didn't bother her and make her go to the buffet, but brought her what she asked for. Tomatoes with mozzarella, smoked trout with horseradish cream, fruit salad with yoghurt and honey—even after the loss of her sense of taste, different foods were different in her mouth when she chewed or bit into them. The way her different children and grandchildren still felt different even after she'd stopped loving them, she thought. If I still enjoy the soft, solid flesh of the trout against the cottony horseradish cream, even just a bit, I should be able to stick it out with my children and grandchildren too. Had Emilia met some boy in the city last night to whom she was now paying attention with the same energy she applied to her grandmother and to her parents' wishes? Yes, she was energetic, strong, diligent. And she also was bighearted. She would make a good doctor.

She stayed in her seat until the tables were being set for lunch. Her face was glowing; she had been sitting in the full sun and had got a little sunburned. She was also a little dazed as she stood up to go into the foyer and settle in an armchair. She fell asleep and woke up to find Emilia sitting on the chair arm wiping the corner of her mouth with a handkerchief.

"Did I dribble in my sleep?"

"You did, Grandmother, but it doesn't matter. I found him."

"You . . ."

"I found Adalbert Paulsen. It was simple—he's in the phone book. I also know he was a professor of philosophy here at the university, and he's a widower and has a daughter who lives in America. The librarian in the philosophy seminar showed me the books he's written—a whole shelf full."

"Let's go home."

"Don't you want to see him? You have to see him! That's why we came here!"

"No, we . . ."

"Perhaps you didn't do it consciously. But trust me, your subconscious brought you here so that you can see him again and forgive each other."

"We're supposed to forgive . . ."

"Yes, you should forgive each other. You need to forgive him for what he did to you. If not, you'll never have peace and nor will he. I'm sure he longs for it and just doesn't trust it'll happen, because you gave him the brush-off in Hamburg back then."

"Leave it be, Emilia. Pack your things. We'll eat lunch on the way."

"I said you'd be there at four."

"You what?"

"I was there, I wanted to know how he lives, and as I was there anyway, I thought I could arrange for you to come and see him. He was a bit hesitant, like you, but then he agreed. I think he's happy you're coming. He's all curious."

"Those are two different things. No, child, this wasn't a good idea of yours. You can call him and cancel, or I simply won't go. I don't want to see him."

But Emilia wouldn't give up. What did she have to lose, it would all be a big win, didn't she feel she was still bitter and mustn't stay that way, didn't she understand that when you can

do some good and forgive someone, you have to do it, wasn't
she at least curious, and this was the last adventure she'd have
in her life. Emilia talked and talked until her grandmother was
exhausted. She could not bear this child with all her belief in
herself and her psychological platitudes and her psychothera-
peutic mission for one minute longer. So she gave in.

9

Emilia offered to drive her, but she preferred to take a taxi. She
didn't want any last instructions. As she got out and walked
to the modest one-family house from the sixties, she became
quite calm. For this he had left her? He may have made it to
professor—but he'd become a petit bourgeois. Or had he always been one?

He opened the door. She recognized his face, the dark eyes,
the bushy eyebrows, the thick hair, now white, the sharp nose
and wide mouth. He was taller than she remembered, thin, and
the suit with the left sleeve tucked into the left pocket hung on
his body as if on a rack. He gave a faint smile. "Nina!"

"It wasn't my idea. My granddaughter Emilia thought I . . ."

"Come in. And then you can explain to me why you don't
want to be here." He went ahead and she followed him down
a hall and through a room full of books out onto the terrace.
There was a view over fruit trees and meadows to the wooded
slope of a mountain. He saw her astonishment. "I didn't like
the house either till I was standing on the terrace." He straightened a chair for her, poured tea for them both, and sat down
opposite her. "Why don't you want to be here?"

She couldn't interpret his smile. Mocking? Embarrassed?
Pitying? "I don't know. The idea of ever seeing you again was

unendurable. But finally perhaps the idea itself was only a habit. But I had it."

"How come your granddaughter decided you ought to see me again?"

"Oh"—she made a dismissive gesture—"I told her about our summer. She had such idiotic ideas about life and love back then that I let myself be pulled in."

"What did you tell her about our summer?" He wasn't smiling anymore.

"What are you asking? You were there, at the doctors' ball and the kiss at the door and in the room in the guesthouse." She was getting angry. "And on the platform and it was you who got on the train and you who left and were never heard from again."

He nodded. "How long did you wait in vain?"

"I don't remember how many days and weeks. But it was an eternity, I do know that."

He looked at her sadly. "It wasn't even ten days, Nina. After ten days I came back and was told by your landlady that you'd moved out. A young man had come to get you, he'd loaded your things into a car, and driven off with you."

"You're lying!" She flew at him.

"No, Nina, I'm not lying."

"Are you trying to knock the ground out from under me? Make me lose faith in my mind and my memory? Make me crazy? How can you say such things?"

He leaned back and ran a hand over his face and head. "Do you remember where I was going when I left?"

"No, I don't remember. But I do remember you never wrote and never called and . . ."

"I went to a philosophical congress in Budapest and couldn't phone you from there or write to you, either. It was the Cold

War and because I wasn't supposed to be there, I couldn't get in touch from there, either. I told you all that."

"I remember you took a trip you didn't have to take. But that's how you were, first came your philosophy, then there was a long gap, then came your colleagues and your friends, and then came me."

"That's not true, either, Nina. I was working like a maniac on my dissertation back then because I wanted to finish, find a job, and marry you. You wanted to be married, that much was clear, and the boy from Hamburg was always ahead by a nose. Didn't you know each other from your childhood? Weren't your families friends and he was your father's assistant?"

"That's as false as everything else you're saying. My father gave him advice about his studies and practical training, because he liked him, but his assistant—no, my husband was never my father's assistant."

He looked at her wearily. "Were you afraid you would fall out of your bourgeois world and land in my poor one? That with me you wouldn't have the things you were used to and needed? I stood outside your parents' house in Hamburg—was that it?"

"What are you trying to do: turn me into some spoiled bourgeois brat? I loved you and you destroyed it all and now you don't want to know anymore."

He said nothing, turned his head away, and looked across the meadows to the mountains. Her eyes followed his, and she saw sheep grazing in the meadow. "Sheep!"

"I was just counting them. Do you remember how angry I could get? I probably managed to frighten you that way too. I can still get really angry, and counting sheep helps."

She tried unsuccessfully to recall any of his outbursts. Her husband, yes, her husband could turn her to ice with his cold rage. If he kept it up for days on end, he drove her to complete despair. "Did you yell at me?"

He didn't reply. Instead he asked, "Will you tell me about your life? I know that you're divorced; I saw your husband's picture in the newspaper on his eightieth birthday with another woman. His children were in the picture too—are they yours?"

"Do you want me to say my life went wrong, and I should have waited for you back then?"

He laughed. She remembered how she'd loved his uninhibited peals of laughter and how they'd also startled her. She realized he wasn't just laughing at her question, he was laughing to dissipate the tension. But what was so funny about her question?

"I've written things about that, about how life's really big decisions aren't right or wrong, it's just that one lives different lives. No, I don't think your life went wrong."

10

She talked. She'd given up her studies, because her husband needed her. He had got a job as a senior physician, although he had no doctorate; it was assumed he would remedy that as fast as possible. Besides which, he had taken on the editing of an important professional journal. She wrote and line-edited for him. "I was good. Helmut's successor offered me a job as assistant editor. But Helmut told him it would have to wait till I was a merry widow."

Then the children came. They arrived quickly one after the other, and if there hadn't been complications with the fourth, there would have been more. "You have a daughter—I don't know how you did it, but with four children there was absolutely no question of picking up my studies again. I had my hands full. But it was also great to watch the children grow up and make something of themselves. The eldest is a judge in the federal court, the next is a museum director, and the girls are housewives and mothers like me, but one is married to a professor and the other to a conductor. I have thirteen grand-children—do you have some too?"

He shook his head. "My daughter isn't married and has no children. She's a little autistic."

"What was your wife like?"

"She was almost as tall and thin as I am. She wrote poetry—wonderful, crazy, despairing poetry. I love the poems, although I don't often understand them. I also didn't understand the depressions Julia battled her whole life long. Or what triggered them and what ended them, if there was some rhythm of the moon or the sun that played a role, or the things she ate and drank."

"But she didn't kill herself!"

"No, she died of cancer."

She nodded. "After me you looked for someone completely different. I wish I'd read more in my life, but for the longest time all I read were the things I had to edit and then the other things I wanted to read because they were what the children were reading and I wanted to be able to talk to them about them—so I got out of the habit. I should have plenty of time now, but what would I do with anything once I'd read it?"

"I was standing in the kitchen as you came up the short path from the street to the house, and I recognized your step immediately. You walk as firmly as you ever did. Clack, clack, clack—I've never met a woman who walks with such determination. Back then I thought you were as determined as your walk was."

"And back then I thought you'd lead me as lightly and safely through life as you led me when we were dancing."

"I would like to have lived the way I danced. Julia didn't dance."

"Were you happy with her? Are you happy about your life?"

He breathed deeply in and out and leaned back. "I can no longer imagine life without her. I also can't imagine any life other than the one I have. Of course I can figure out this possibility or that, but it's all abstract."

"That's not how it is with me. I'm always imagining things differently from the way they happened. What if I'd finished my degree and then worked? If I'd actually taken on the job as assistant editor? If I'd got a divorce from Helmut when he had his first affair? If I'd raised the children less seriously and severely and allowed them to be more chaotic and happy? If I'd seen life as more than a mechanism of duties and responsibilities? If you hadn't left me?"

"I . . ." He stopped.

She'd had to say it again. But she didn't want a fight and she didn't want to anger him and asked, "Will I be able to understand the things you've written? I'd like to try."

"I'll send you something that may perhaps interest you. Will you give me your address?"

She opened her purse and gave him a card.

"Thank you." He held it in his hand. "I never got as far as having cards in my life."

She laughed. "It's not too late." She stood up. "Would you be kind enough to call a taxi?"

She followed him into his study. It was next to the room with the terrace and had the same view of the mountains. While he was on the telephone, she looked around. The walls here too were crammed with bookcases, the desk covered in books and papers, on one side a table with a computer, on the other a bulletin board full of bills, claim tickets, newspaper clippings, handwritten notes, photographs. The tall, gaunt woman with the sad eyes must be Julia, the younger woman with the closed expression his daughter. In one picture a black dog with eyes as sad as Julia's gazed into the camera. In another Adalbert, in a black suit, stood next to other men in black suits, as if they were all a school class late for their leaving exams. The man in uniform and the woman dressed as a nurse standing outside a front door must be Adalbert's parents.

Then she saw the little black-and-white photo of him and her. They were standing on a platform in each other's arms. It couldn't be . . . She shook her head.

He put down the receiver and came to stand next to her. "No, that's not when we were saying goodbye. We picked you up at the station once, your friend Elena, my friend Eberhard, and I. It was late afternoon and we all went to the river and had a picnic. Eberhard had inherited a wind-up gramophone from his grandfather and found some old 78 records at a junk dealer's and we danced into the night. Do you remember?"

"Did that picture always hang next to your desk?"

He shook his head. "Not in the first years. But since then. The taxi will be here any minute."

They went out to the street. "Do you take care of the garden?"

"No, a gardener does that. I prune the roses."

"Thank you," she said, put her arms around him and felt his bones. "Are you healthy? You're nothing but skin and bones."

He put his right arm around her and held her. "Look after yourself, Nina."

Then the taxi came. Adalbert held open the door, helped her in, and closed the door behind her. She turned around and saw him standing there, getting smaller and smaller.

11

Emilia had been waiting in the foyer. She leapt to her feet and ran to meet her. "How was it?"

"I'll tell you tomorrow while we're driving. All I want to do now is have supper and go to a movie."

They ate on the terrace in the inner courtyard. It was early, they were the first guests, and the square of houses protected them from the sounds of the street and of traffic. A blackbird was singing on a roof, the bells rang at seven o'clock, otherwise everything was still. Emilia was rather hurt and didn't want to talk, so they ate in silence.

She didn't care what kind of film she saw. She hadn't been to a cinema very often in her life and had never got used to television. But she found the bright, moving images on the big screen overwhelming, and this was an evening when she wanted to be overwhelmed. The film achieved this, but not in a way that made her forget everything; it made her remember—dreams she dreamed as a child, her longing for something bigger and more wonderful than her everyday life of family and school, her pathetic attempts to find it in ballet and the piano. The little boy whose story they were watching was fascinated by film, gave the man in the little Sicilian village who ran the projector no peace till he let him help in the projection room and finally become a director. In the end the only one of her childhood dreams that survived was the dream of finding the right man, and she hadn't managed to do that, either.

But she had never allowed herself self-pity and she wasn't going to allow it today, either. Emilia came out of the movie theater with tears in her eyes, put her arms around her, and held her close. She patted Emilia's back soothingly; she couldn't bring herself to put her own arm around her granddaughter. Emilia soon let go again and they walked side by side through the city in the bright summer evening to the hotel.

"You really want to go home tomorrow?"

"I don't have to be back early, so we don't have to set off early. Is breakfast at nine okay?"

Emilia nodded. But she wasn't happy with her grandmother and the last two days. "You're going to sleep now as if nothing had happened?"

She laughed. "Even if nothing happened, I don't sleep as if nothing happened. You know, when you're young, you're either asleep or wide awake and up and about. When you're old, there's a third possibility: the nights when you're neither asleep nor awake and up and about. It's a state all its own, and one of the secrets of getting old is to accept it as such. Why don't you go for a wander through the city again if you want, I'll allow you."

She went up to her room and got into bed, arming herself for a night of sleeping and waking and remembering and thinking and sleeping and waking again. But when she woke up, it was morning.

Then they were in the car, driving along the little road again, following the winding river. It had dawned on Emilia that her questions were getting her nowhere, so she'd stopped asking. She waited.

"It wasn't the way I told you on the drive here. He didn't leave me. I left him." That basically was it. But for Emilia's sake she kept talking. "When we said goodbye at the station, I knew he'd be coming back soon, and also that he wouldn't be able to write or call. I could have waited for him. But my parents had found out that I wasn't doing any practical training course, and sent Helmut. He was to bring me home, and he did. I was afraid of life with Adalbert, of the fact that he'd grown up in poverty and didn't care, of his mind, which I couldn't follow, and of the break with my parents. Helmut was my world, and I ran back to that world."

12

"Why did you tell me a different story?"

"I believed it had all happened differently. Even while I was talking to Adalbert."

"But you can't just . . ."

"Yes, Emilia, you can. I couldn't bear it, that I made the wrong decision. Adalbert says there are no wrong decisions—I couldn't bear it that I'd decided the way I'd decided. And did I decide at all? What I felt back then was that I was being pulled first toward Adalbert and then even more strongly back into my old world and to Helmut. When I wasn't happy in that old world and with Helmut, I didn't forgive Adalbert for not see-ing my fear and helping me, and not holding on to me. I felt abandoned by him and my memory turned this into the entire scene when he said goodbye on the platform."

"But you were the one who decided!"

She didn't know how to answer. That it didn't make any dif-ference, because she'd had to live with the consequences one way or the other? That she didn't actually know what making decisions meant? After Helmut had brought her home, it was a given that she was going to marry him, it was a given that the children would be born, and it was a given that he would have affairs. The duties she had lived for were there and had to be fulfilled—where was the decision in that?

Irritated, she said, "Should I have decided not to take care of the children? Not to look after them when they were sick, not to talk about what was on their minds, not to take them to concerts and plays, not to find the right schools, and not to help with their homework? And with you grandchildren—should I have neglected my duties—"

"Your duties? Are we just duties to you? Were your children just duties for you?"

"No, I love you all, of course. I . . ."

"That sounds as if love to you is just another duty."

She felt Emilia was interrupting her too often. At the same time she didn't know what to say next. They left the country road and threaded their way into the heavy traffic on the Autobahn. Emilia drove fast, faster than she had on the way down, and sometimes recklessly, without paying attention.

"Please, can you slow down? It's making me afraid."

Emilia swerved alarmingly into the slow lane between two trundling trucks. "Happy?"

She was tired, didn't want to sleep, but dropped off nonetheless. She dreamed she was a little girl walking through a city holding her mother's hand. Although she knew the houses and the streets, she felt like a stranger in the city. That, she thought in the dream, is because I'm still little. But it didn't help; the further they walked, the more oppressed and anxious she became. Then she was terrified by a big black dog with big black eyes, and she woke up with a cry of alarm.

"Something the matter, Grandmother?"

"I was dreaming." She saw on a road sign that it wasn't much further to home. While she was asleep Emilia had switched back into the fast lane again.

"I'm going to bring you home and then take off."

"To your parents?"

"No. I don't have to be home to wait for news of whether I've got a place at the university or not. I have a little money and I'm going to visit my girlfriend in Costa Rica. I've always wanted to learn Spanish."

"But this evening . . ."

"This evening I'm driving to Frankfurt and I'll stay with another girlfriend until I get a flight."

She felt she should say something, either encouraging or by way of a warning. But she couldn't think that fast. Was Emilia doing things right or wrong? She admired Emilia's decisiveness, but she couldn't say that without knowing that it was the right thing to do.

After Emilia had brought her home and packed, she took her to the bus stop. "Thank you. Without you I wouldn't have got well again. And without you I wouldn't have made the trip."

Emilia shrugged. "No problem."

"I've disappointed you, haven't I?" She searched for words to make it all right again. But she didn't find any. "You make things better." The bus came, she took Emilia in her arms, and Emilia did the same. She climbed into the bus in front and took some time to work her way to the back. Before the bus disappeared around the curve in the road, she knelt up on the backseat and waved.

13

The fine summer weather continued. In the evenings there were often storms, and she would sit out on the covered balcony to watch the clouds darken, the wind bend the trees, and the drops begin to fall, one by one at first, then in torrents. When the temperature dropped, she would cover herself with a blanket. Sometimes she fell asleep, waking only when it was night. On mornings after the storms, the air was intoxicatingly fresh.

She lengthened her walks and made plans to take a trip, but couldn't decide where. Emilia sent a postcard from Costa Rica. Emilia's parents hadn't forgiven her for letting Emilia go. She should at least have insisted on being given the address of the girlfriend in Frankfurt, so they could have located her before she flew and talked to her. Finally she said she didn't want to hear another word on the subject, and if they couldn't stop talking about it, please, would they stop coming to visit.

After a few weeks a little package arrived from Adalbert. She liked the slender book bound in black linen; she liked looking at it and picking it up. She also liked the title: *Hope and Decision*. But she didn't really want to know what Adalbert thought.

What she really would have liked to know was if he still danced so well. How could it be otherwise? When she'd visited him, she should have stayed a little while, turned on the radio, and danced with him, out of the room and onto the terrace, his arm leading her as safely and as lightly as if she were floating.

FLIGHTS OF LOVE

In these seven stories, Bernhard Schlink's characters—men with importunate appetites and unfortunate habits of deception—are uneasily suspended between the desire for love and the impulse toward flight. A young boy's fascination with an eerily erotic painting gradually leads him into the labyrinth of his family's secrets. The friendship between a West Berliner and an idealistic young couple from the East founders amid the prosperity and revelations that follow the collapse of communism. An acrobatic philanderer (one wife and two mistresses, all apparently quite happy) begins to crack under the weight of his abundance. By turns brooding and comic, filled with the suspense that comes from the inexorable unfolding of character, *Flights of Love* is nothing less than masterful.

Fiction/Short Stories

THE GORDIAN KNOT

Georg Polger ekes out a lonely living as a freelance translator in the south of France, until he is approached by a certain Mr. Bulnakov, who has an intriguing proposition: Georg is to take over a local translation agency and finish a project left by the previous owner, who died in a mysterious accident. The money is right, and then there is the matter of Bulnakov's secretary, Francoise, with whom Georg has fallen hopelessly in love. Late one night, however, Georg discovers Francoise secretly photographing a sensitive military project. He is shocked and heartbroken. Then, her eventual disappearance leaves him not only bereft, but suspicious of the motivations behind Mr. Bulnakov's offer. To make matters worse, Georg's every move is being watched. Determined to find out who Francoise really is, and to foil whoever is tracking him, Georg sets out on an mission that will take him to New York City, where with each step he is dragged deeper and deeper into a deadly whirlpool in which friend and foe are indistinguishable.

Fiction/Thriller

HOMECOMING

Growing up with his mother in Germany, Peter Debauer knows little about his father, an apparent victim of the Second World War. But when he stumbles upon a few pages from a long-lost novel, Peter embarks on a quest that leads him across Europe to the United States, chasing fragments of a story within a story and a master of disguises who may or may not exist. *Homecoming* is a tale of fathers and sons, men and women, war and peace. It reveals the humanity that survives the trauma of war and the ongoing possibility for redemption.

Fiction/Literature

THE READER

Hailed for its coiled eroticism and the moral claims it makes upon the reader, this mesmerizing novel is a story of love and secrets, horror and compassion, unfolding against the haunted landscape of postwar Germany. When he falls ill on his way home from school, fifteen-year-old Michael Berg is rescued by Hanna, a woman twice his age. In time she becomes his lover—then she inexplicably disappears. When Michael next sees her, he is a young law student, and she is on trial for a hideous crime. As he watches her refuse to defend her innocence, Michael gradually realizes that Hanna may be guarding a secret she considers more shameful than murder.

Fiction/Literature

ALSO AVAILABLE FROM VINTAGE CRIME/BLACK LIZARD

Self's Deception
Self's Murder
Self's Punishment
The Weekend

VINTAGE INTERNATIONAL
Available wherever books are sold.
www.vintagebooks.com